N.B.

X
K

(

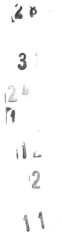

20

3

24
1

1

2

11

To

Coventry Cit

'You've built yourself a cocoon. If you love, then you get hurt.'

'Oh, please,' she whispered. 'What's with the psychoanalysis?'

'I did it as a minor during med,' he said, suddenly cheerful. 'I knew it'd come in handy some day.'

'I'm not your patient.'

'No,' he said, and his voice was serious again. 'You're my love. You're my Ally. You're a wonderful doctor and a wonderful massage therapist and a wonderful daughter and karate expert and toast-maker and floor-scrubber. But most of all you're you. I love you, Ally. Whoever you are. Whatever you do.'

'You're crazy.'

Marion Lennox is a country girl, born on a south-east Australian dairy farm. She moved on—mostly because the cows just weren't interested in her stories! Married to a 'very special doctor', Marion writes hugely popular Medical Romances®. In her other life she cares for kids, cats, dogs, chooks and goldfish. She travels, she fights her rampant garden (she's losing) and her house dust (she's lost!)—oh, and she teaches statistics and computing to undergraduates at her local university. Marion Lennox also writes for Tender Romance® and has won awards for her writing in Australia, New Zealand and the USA.

Recent titles by the same author:

THE DOCTOR'S RESCUE MISSION
THE POLICE DOCTOR'S SECRET
BUSHFIRE BRIDE
IN DOCTOR DARLING'S CARE

THE DOCTOR'S SPECIAL TOUCH

BY
MARION LENNOX

MILLS & BOON®

First published in Great Britain 2005
Large Print edition 2005
Harlequin Mills & Boon Limited,
Eton House, 18-24 Paradise Road,
Richmond, Surrey TW9 1SR

© Marion Lennox 2005

ISBN 0 263 18487 0

Set in Times Roman 15¼ on 17 pt.
17-1205-55438

Printed and bound in Great Britain
by Antony Rowe Ltd, Chippenham, Wiltshire

CHAPTER ONE

'ARE you out of your mind?'

Ally's ladder wobbled to the point of peril.

Until now, the main street of Tambrine Creek had been deserted. At eight a.m. on a glorious autumn morning, anyone without any urgent occupation was walking on the beach, pottering on the jetty or simply sitting in the sun, soaking up the warmth before winter.

Which left Ally alone in Main Street. It was gorgeous even there, she'd decided as she worked. The shopping precinct of the tiny harbour town was lined with oaks—trees that had been acorns when Ally's great-grandfather had first sailed his fishing boat into the harbour a hundred years before. Now the oaks were at their best, their leaves ranging from vivid green to deep, glorious crimson. They were starting to drop, turning the street into a rainbow of autumn colour.

Which was why Ally had a leaf above her eye right now, caught by her honey-blonde fringe. She'd been in the process of brushing it away when the stranger had spoken.

And shocked her into almost falling off her ladder.

She was brushing the leaf from her fringe. She was holding a paintpot, with her brush balanced on the top. That didn't leave a lot of hands to clutch her ladder. But clutching the ladder was suddenly a priority. She made a grab, subconsciously deciding whether to drop the leaf or the paintpot.

Which one? According to Murphy's law, some things were inevitable.

So the pot fell, and it hit street level right at the stranger's feet. A mass of sky-blue paint shot out over the pavement, over the leaves—over the stranger's shoes.

Whoa!

Safely clutching her ladder—she'd finally decided maybe she could release her leaf as well—Ally surveyed the scene below with dismay.

The guy underneath was gorgeous. Seriously gorgeous, in a sort of any-excuse-to-put-him-on-the-front-page-of-a-women's-magazine-type gorgeous. Tall, broad-shouldered, with a lovely strong-boned face. Deep, dark grey eyes. Wavy, russet hair, a bit too long. Yep, gorgeous.

The clothes helped, too. The man was dressed relatively formally for this laid-back seaside village in neat, tailored trousers and a short-sleeved shirt in rich cream linen. The man had taste. And he was wearing a tie, for heaven's sake—and not a bad tie either, she conceded.

What else? He had lovely shoes. Brogues. Quality. Beautifully streaked now with sky-blue paint.

His shoes seemed to be a cause for concern. Ally clutched her ladder and sought valiantly for something to say.

Finally she found it. She let the word ring around her head a little, just to see how it sounded. Not great, she thought, but she couldn't think of much else. He'd scared her. Don't launch straight into grovelling apology, she told herself. So what was left?

'Whoops,' she said.

Whoops.

The word hung in the early morning stillness. The stranger stared for a bit longer at his shoes—as if his feet had personally let him down—and then he turned his attention back to her.

Involuntarily Ally's hands clutched even tighter at the ladder. Whew. She was about to get a blast. His deep, grey-flecked eyes looked straight up at her, and they blazed with anger.

This man intended to let her have it with both barrels.

OK. She knew about anger. She'd lived through it before and she could live with it again. She closed her eyes and braced herself.

Silence. Then: 'Hey, I'm not going to hit you,' he told her.

That was out of left field. She opened her eyes cautiously and peered down.

'I beg your pardon?'

'I said I'm not about to hit you,' he told her. 'Or knock you off your ladder. So you can stop looking like that. Much as you deserve it, there's no way painting shoes merits physical violence.'

She thought about that and decided she agreed. She agreed entirely. She shouldn't expect violence, she thought, but she had entirely the wrong slant on the world, and she'd had it for ever.

'You scared me,' she said, still cautious.

'So I did.' His voice was almost cordial. 'Silly me. So you decided to paint me in return.'

'It might come off,' she told him. 'With turpentine.'

'Do you have turpentine?'

'No.'

He sighed. 'You're painting with oil-based paint—and you don't have turpentine?'

'I'll get some. When the store opens.'

'At nine o'clock. By which time my shoes will be dry. Blue and dry.'

'But I've only just started to paint, so I don't need turpentine yet. Or I didn't.' She gazed up at her handiwork then down to his shoes, and her ladder wobbled again.

'You know, if I were you I'd come down,' he told her. 'That ladder isn't safe. You need someone holding the bottom.' Then, as if it occurred to him that she just might ask him to volunteer, he added, 'Maybe you need to get a different type of ladder.'

'This one's fine.' Though maybe he did have a point, she conceded. It was sort of wobbly. Sort of very wobbly. Maybe instead of one that balanced against the shop front, she should get one that was self-supporting.

How much did a self-supporting ladder cost?

Probably far too much. How much did she have left in the kitty? About forty dollars to last until she got her first client.

But he was still worrying. 'You'll kill yourself,' he told her. 'Come down.'

She considered this and found a flaw. 'The pavement's all blue,' she told him. 'I might get my shoes dirty.'

'Lady...'

'Mmm?' She dared a smile and discovered he was trying not to smile back. She smiled a little more—just to see—and the corners of his mouth couldn't help themselves. They curved upward and the flecked grey eyes twinkled.

Whew! It was some smile. A killer smile.

The sort of smile that made a girl clutch her ladder again.

But the smile had moved on. 'Whoever's employing you should be sued for making you work with a ladder like this.' He gazed up at the sign she'd etched in pencil and was now filling in with paint. 'And to get back to my first point...'

'Which was asking me was I out of my mind.'

'You're painting a sign,' he said. 'Advertising a doctor's rooms. Right next to my surgery.'

'Your surgery?'

He pointed sideways. She peered sideways and wobbled again.

He sighed. He caught the ladder and held it firmly on each side, gaining a liberal coating of blue paint on each hand as he did.

'Get down,' he told her. 'Right now. I'm the Dr Darcy Rochester of the small, insignificant bronze plate on the next-door clinic. A nice, discreet little doctor's sign. As opposed to your monstrosity.'

'Monstrosity?'

'Monstrosity. Signs four feet high are a definite monstrosity. And painting them above eye level is ridiculous. For both of us. I don't want another patient,' he told her. 'I'm worked off my feet as it is, and this is a one-doctor town. If you break your neck you're in real trouble.'

'I might be at that,' she admitted. She thought about what he'd said, sorting it out in her head. Figuring out what was important. 'You're the Dr Darcy Rochester in the sign?'

'Yes.'

Nice. She'd been wondering what he looked like, imagining who he could be, and this was perfect. He so fitted his name.

'Has anyone ever told you that you have a very romantic name?'

'They have, as a matter of fact,' he said with exaggerated patience. 'My mother was a romance addict. She couldn't believe her luck when she met Sam Rochester. She called my brother—'

'Don't tell me. Edward?'

'Nothing so boring. Try Byron.' Then, at her look of horror, he grinned. 'He calls himself Brian and anyone who uses Byron gets slugged. You know, with the amount of paint sprayed on these rungs, if I stay holding this ladder for much longer I'm going to stick here. Get down. Now.'

She didn't have much choice. She took a deep breath and descended. With care. Another leaf landed on her nose and she blew it aside. It distracted her, but not very much.

He was too near. Too close. And when she took those last couple of steps he was right behind her. He was big, warm and solid, with the faint scent of something incredibly masculine emanating from his person. Like open fires. Woodsmoke.

'Do you smoke?' she demanded, and he was so surprised that he took a step back. Breaking the intimacy. Which was good.

Wasn't it?

'Um…no.'

'You smell like smoke.'

'You smell like paint thinner,' he told her, trying not to smile. 'I don't ask if you drink it.'

'Sorry.' She bit her lip. 'Of course. It's none of my business. But if you're a doctor…'

'I have a wood stove in my kitchen,' he said, with the resigned tolerance he might have used if she'd been a too-inquisitive child. 'I cook my morning toast on a toasting fork.'

Her eyes widened. That brought back memories. 'Really?'

'Really.'

'Cool.'

But he'd moved on. Back to business. 'You know, I really would like to know what your sign means,' he told her. 'We seem to be going the long way round here. You know what I do. You know about my crazy mother's addiction to romance.

You know I cook my toast on a wood stove.' His voice lowered, and suddenly the laughter was gone. 'So now it's your turn. Are you going to tell me why on earth there is a blue sign half written on the building next door to mine saying ''Dr A. J. Westruther''?'

She gulped. Dr A. J. Westruther. She'd agonised over whether to use the 'Doctor' bit. But she was entitled, and if it meant more clients…

This was a small country town and massage would be a new experience for most. If the label 'Doctor' made the locals feel more comfortable— and scared away those for whom massage meant something totally inappropriate—why shouldn't she use it?

'Dr Westruther's me,' she told him.

This conversation had been frivolous up to now. But suddenly it wasn't. She wiped her hands on the sides of her paint-stained overalls and thought, Uh-oh. Here goes.

'You're Dr Westruther?'

'Ally,' she told him and put out her hand.

He didn't take it.

'No one's employing you to paint a sign?'

'No.'

'You're saying that you're a doctor?'

'Yep.'

His brows hiked in disbelief. 'You're a doctor—and you're setting up in opposition to me?'

'Oh, come on.' She tried to smile but there was something about the sudden shadowing of this man's eyes that made her smile fade before it formed. 'You think I'd do that? It'd be crazy to set up in opposition.'

'You're a...dentist, then?' His eyes raked hers, and she saw disbelief that she could be anything so sensible. So mature.

This was hardly the way she'd wanted to meet this man, she thought. If this worked out, she hoped that maybe he could send work her way. That was why she'd rented this place so close to the doctor's surgery. But when she'd visited the town two weeks ago to organise a rental, a locum had been working in Dr Darcy Rochester's rooms. The gangly locum who'd been filling in for him had said that he'd tell...Darcy about her, but maybe he hadn't.

As a professional approach, this was now really difficult. She'd imagined a cool, collected visit to his surgery, wearing one of her remaining decent suits, pulling her hair back into a twist that made her look almost as old as her twenty-nine years, maybe even wearing glasses. Handing him her card.

It hadn't happened like that. She hadn't been able to afford cards. She was aware that she looked about twelve. Her overalls were disgusting. Her long blonde hair was hauled back into two pigtails to keep it free from paint, and she was wearing no make-up. And he was angry and confused.

She had to make things right. Somehow.

'I'm not a dentist,' she told him. 'Urk. All those teeth.' She grimaced and hauled the ladder along past where she'd been working so he could see what the final sign would be.

After the huge, blue sign—Dr A. J. Westruther—was another, as yet only faintly stencilled in pencil.

Massage Therapist.

'You're a masseur,' he said blankly, and she nodded. There was something in his voice that warned her to stay noncommittal. Let him make the judgements here.

'You're setting up professional rooms as a *masseur.*'

That was enough. 'Hey, we're not talking red-light district,' she snapped. There was enough disdain in his voice to make it perfectly plain what his initial reaction was. 'I give remedial and relaxation massage, and I do it professionally. By the way, I'm a masseuse. Not a masseur. Get your sexes right.'

'Let's get the qualifications right.' Anger met anger. 'You're calling yourself a doctor?'

'Yes!' Her eyes blazed. Heck, she was committed to this profession. She'd fallen into it sideways but she loved it. She loved that she was able to help people. Finally. And she didn't need this man's condemnation. It'd be great if he supported her but she'd gather clients without him.

'It's illegal to call yourself a doctor.'

'Phone my university,' she snapped. 'Check my qualifications.'

'Doctor of what?'

'Go jump.' She was suddenly overpoweringly angry. Overpoweringly weary. What business was it of this man what her qualifications were? She was telling no lies. She wasn't misrepresenting herself.

Maybe it had been a mistake to use the word 'doctor' in her sign. She'd agonised over it but, heck, she'd abandoned so much. If the use of one word would help her build this new career—this new life—then use it she would.

So much else had been taken from her. They couldn't take this.

'Look,' she said wearily, her anger receding. Anger solved nothing. She knew that. 'We're getting off to a really bad start here. I've tossed blue paint at you and you've implied I'm a hooker.'

'I didn't.'

'You did. If you check, you'll find that I'm absolutely entitled to use the title "Doctor".'

'You don't think a doctorate—of what, basket weaving?—might be just a bit misleading when you're setting up in a medical precinct?'

'Medical precinct?' She swallowed more anger. Or tried to. Then she gazed around. There were a total of five shops in the tiny township of Tambrine Creek. Then there was a pub and a petrol station. The oak-lined main street ran straight down to the harbour, where the fishing boats moored and sold their fish from the final shop—a fishermen's co-op that had existed for generations.

'You know, we're not talking Harley Street here,' she ventured. 'Medical precinct? I don't think so.'

'There's two premises.'

'Yeah, two medical premises. Yours and mine. Yours is a doctor's surgery. Mine is a massage centre. It was a tearoom once, but it's been closed for twenty years. The owner's thrilled to get rent from me and the council has no objection to me setting up. So what's your problem? Do I somehow downgrade your neighbourhood?'

'There's no need to be angry.'

'It's not me who's angry,' she told him, but she was lying. She'd done with the placating. 'Basket weaving,' she muttered. 'I wish it had been purple paint I threw at you and I wish it had hit your head. Now, are you going to sue me for painting your feet? If so, there's no lawyer in town but I can't commend you strongly enough to leave town and find one. Preferably one in another state. I need to get on with my work.'

'You've spilled your paint.'

'Of course I have,' she snapped. 'And it was well worth it. Your brogues are drying, Dr Rochester. You need to go find some turpentine.'

'You'll never make a living.'

'We'll see.' She stooped to lift her now empty paintpot from the pavement and was suddenly aware that someone was watching them. An elderly lady, a basket on one arm and a poodle dangling from the other, was gazing at the pair of them as if she couldn't believe her eyes.

'It's Ally,' she whispered. 'Ally Lindford. You've come home!'

Crimplene was very hard to escape, especially when Crimplene was intent on smothering you. Ally was enfolded in a bosom so ample she'd never felt anything like it, and it took her a few valiant tries before she could finally find enough space to breathe.

Doris Kerr. How could she have forgotten Doris?

She hadn't. She hadn't forgotten a single person in this town.

So who was this Dr Rochester? she wondered from her cocoon of Crimplene. Definitely a newcomer. But maybe not so new. Ally had been away for twenty years.

'I saw the Dr A starting on the wall when I walked my Chloe last night.' Doris had decided to take pity on her and hold her at arm's length. 'And I said to myself—a doctor? Yes. Just what we need. Dr Rochester needs help so much. But then I saw the pencilling saying massage and I said to myself we don't need a massage parlour here— that's the last thing we want in a respectable town like this—and I phoned Fred on the town council before I went to bed. But he said it's not like I think—it's a proper nice massage that you get when you hurt yourself and then he told me who it was who'd applied to run it and I was so excited. I thought I'd come down this very morning to see for myself and… Oh, my dear, it is so good to see you again.'

The Crimplene flooded toward her again and Ally managed to give Darcy a despairing glance before she was once again enfolded.

'Um… It seems you two know each other,' Darcy said.

'Mmph.' It was all Ally could manage.

'And you're using your grandpa's name,' Doris was saying. 'Dr Westruther. How wonderful is that? I never did like Lindford. Evil is as evil does and…' She caught herself. 'Well, he was your father and he's long dead so maybe I shouldn't be speaking ill of him. But if your poor mother had just decided to go back to using Westruther…' She gulped and hauled back, still hanging onto Ally but beaming across at Darcy. 'Isn't this just wonderful? A Dr Westruther in Tambrine Creek again after all these years.'

'She's a masseur,' Darcy said, and Ally glowered.

'Don't say it like I'm a dung beetle.'

'Oh, I'm sure he doesn't mean it, dear,' Doris told her. 'He's the best thing since sliced bread is our Dr Rochester. Do you know, we didn't have a doctor for five years before he came. And he's so nice.'

'I can see that,' Ally agreed.

'I did hold the ladder,' he told her. 'And I got blue hands.'

'You scared me.'

'Your grandpa was the doctor here?'

'Grandpa died seventeen years ago.'

'That's when Ally left town,' Doris told him. 'Her father came and took her away. Nothing we could say made any difference. But…he looked after you, didn't he, lass?'

'He looked after me,' Ally agreed tightly.

'And now you're back.'

'I am.' She made a determined effort to regain control—to pin a cheerful smile on her face and move forward. 'And I'm here to stay.'

'Where are you living?'

'Here. Above the shop.'

'You can't do that.' Doris seemed horrified.

'Of course I can.' How to explain to Doris that it was palatial compared to some of the places she'd lived in? 'And now I've met the neighbour and he's such a sweetheart.'

'He is nice,' Doris said, but she'd caught the tone of Ally's voice and she was starting to sound dubious. 'You two don't sound as if you've started off on the right foot.'

'She threw blue paint at my feet,' Darcy said.

'I'm sure she didn't.' Doris looked from one to the other—and then to Ally's ladder. 'You know, that doesn't look all that safe to me, love.'

'Just what I was saying.' Darcy sounded almost triumphant.

'Tell you what.' Doris was clearly thinking on her feet. 'The fleet's in at the moment. Old Charlie

Hammer's funeral's this afternoon so the fisher-men can't go out until they see him buried. And everyone'll be sober until the wake. Why don't I send a few of the men up here to finish your paint-ing for you, dear? And anything else you might need doing. You know we all respected your grandpa, and everyone'll be so pleased you're back. And a doctor, too.'

'She's a masseur.' Darcy was starting to sound a little desperate and Ally gave him her nicest, pitying smile.

'Doctors can be massage therapists, too,' she told him. 'And massage therapists can be doctors.'

'Are you telling me you seriously plan to make a living in this town?'

'Of course.'

'No one will come.'

'I will,' Doris said soundly. 'I like a little mas-sage. Not that I've ever had one, of course, but they sound nice. I was telling Henry only the other night that a rub would do me the world of good. Not like those tablets you have me on, Dr Rochester. I'm sure you're doing your best, but Dr Westruther's granddaughter… Ooh, I'm that pleased. And I'm sure Gloria will come as soon as she knows about you—her arthritis is something terrible—and my Beryl, and…everyone. I'll just go and spread the word. It's wonderful, that's what it is. It's just wonderful. Come on, Chloe.'

And with a tug on the unfortunate poodle's leash, she sailed away to spread the word.

Dr Darcy Rochester was left staring at Dr Ally Westruther. Speechless. While she stared at him and tried to decide where to go from there.

'You know, you'd really better go and take that paint off,' Ally said finally. 'We don't want you to stay blue for ever, now, do we?'

'You're a local?'

'Yes.'

'And you're really setting up for massage.'

'That seems to be the intention.'

'That's fine,' he said bluntly. 'But take the ''Doctor'' off the sign. It's misleading.'

'Why is it misleading?'

'I'm the town's doctor.'

'And you don't want anyone else invading your territory?'

'If anyone else wanted to invade, I'd be putting up the white flag before the first shot was fired,' he told her. 'Do you have any idea how big this district is? I'm run off my feet. But you're not going to help.'

No, she thought bleakly. She wasn't. But she may as well reassure him that she wasn't pretending to practise medicine.

'If anyone arrives with broken legs or snakebite, you can be sure I'll send them to you,' she told him. 'As I hope you'll send anyone with muscle soreness to me.'

'You expect me to refer people to you when you call yourself a doctor?'

'Don't be elitist.'

'Don't indulge in deception.'

'I'm not!'

'Look, Ally…'

This was going nowhere. 'I have work to do,' she told him. 'Your paint is drying.'

'You can't do this.'

'Watch me.' She sighed. 'You're just upset because my sign is bigger than yours.'

'Some of us have ethical standards.'

'Well, bully for some of us,' she snapped. 'Now, if you don't mind, I have a sign to write and I've just decided it needs work. It needs to be bigger.'

He stared at her for a long moment. But there was no more to be said. They both knew it.

Finally he turned and stalked up to his surgery door. He disappeared, slamming the door behind him.

He left blue footprints all the way.

Ally was left staring after him. What to do now?

Nothing, she told herself. There was nothing she could do. Just get on with it.

'Whoops,' she said again. She took a deep breath—and then grinned into the morning sun. Whether she had Darcy Rochester's approval or whether she didn't, she was home again and nothing and no one was going to interfere with her happiness.

CHAPTER TWO

THROUGHOUT the next few days Darcy worked on as if she wasn't there. Well, why not? What did a massage therapist have to do with him?

Nothing.

The fact that the entire population was talking about her was none of his business either.

At least he had work to distract him from a woman who was dangerously close to being distracting all by herself.

In truth, he'd seldom been as busy as he was right now. The fine autumn weather broke the afternoon of Charlie Hammer's funeral, meaning the fishing fleet couldn't leave port. The town's fishermen decided *en masse* that if they were in port anyway they may as well kill time getting their assorted ills seen to, swelling his already too-long patient lists.

Then the little community in the hills above the town—alternative lifestylers who didn't believe in getting their children immunised—were hit by an epidemic of chickenpox. As he had three kids with complications and parents who agonised and discussed *ad nauseam* every treatment he advised—

and then refused to let him treat them anyway—
he was going quietly nuts. But going nuts wasn't
on the agenda. If he stopped calmly discussing
treatments with these parents, if he stopped nego-
tiating that at least they keep track of fluid bal-
ances—if he lost his cool—then these kids
wouldn't make it to be insurance salesmen or as-
trophysicists or whatever else kids of dyed-in-the-
wool hippies became if they survived childhood.

Then there was the added complication of the
entire town trooping by to see Ally's much talked-
of new premises. While they were there, they remembered they may just as well pop next door to
the doctor's surgery and make an appointment to
have their sore elbow seen to, or talk about Mum's
Alzheimer's—and see for themselves just how Dr
Rochester was taking this new arrival.

Doris Kerr had obviously spread the fact that
Darcy hadn't reacted with pleasure to Ally's arrival. His reaction had gone down like a lead bal-
loon. Every single patient commented on the hive
of industry next door to his surgery. Many of the
long-term town residents—those who remembered
Ally from childhood—took pains to tell him how
wonderful it was that a little girl they'd clearly
held in affection had finally come home.

And their message was clear. 'Don't mess with Ally Westruther. Even if her sign is bigger than yours.'

Fine. He wouldn't mess with Ally Westruther. He didn't want to think about her. But not thinking about her was impossible, too.

Even among his staff… Betty, his receptionist, got teary-eyed about Ally at least twice a day.

'Oh, Dr Rochester, I'm so pleased to think that little mite has finally found her way home,' she told him. 'And to have another Dr Westruther in town… It seems so right.'

He grimaced but somehow he refrained from saying, 'She's not a doctor.'

He thought it, though.

What had she said? *Contact my university and ask.*

OK, so she probably did have some sort of doctorate, he conceded, and maybe he'd been being petty, suggesting it was in basket weaving. But you couldn't get doctorates in massage. He knew that. He'd checked. He'd checked five minutes after he'd unsuccessfully tried to clean his shoes.

So the doctorate she was using to promote her massage business must be in something esoteric— like the mating habits of North Baluchistan dung beetles or the literary comparison of Byron and Tennyson or…or something, and she couldn't make a living so she'd turned to massage and was using her doctorate to attract patients.

That was a guess, he conceded. Nearly everything was a guess when it came to Ally. As much as the locals were pleased to see her, no one knew what she'd been doing in the last twenty years or so.

'Her mother brought her home to her grandpa when she was tiny,' Betty told him, unasked, as she was sorting patient records he needed for the afternoon. 'There was a really unhappy marriage and her father went to jail. I can't remember all the details but I know old Doc Westruther wouldn't speak of him. Her mother didn't stay very long—she disappeared and no one knew where she went—but when she went she left the little girl behind. Then suddenly the old doc died and her father turned up to claim her. There were so many people who would have taken her in but her father just said, "She's my kid and she comes with me." There was nothing we could do about it. No one knew where her mother was. I remember her father dragging her into a beat-up old jalopy and Sue, her best friend, wailing at the top of her lungs. I saw them leave town. Her little face was pressed against the car's back window and…well, the memory never left me. I wondered and wondered. Her father seemed brutal.'

Brutal. Darcy was trying to concentrate on reading Mrs Skye's patient notes. Elsie Skye's gout had been playing up and she was coming to see him for the third time. If the treatment he had her on wasn't working then he needed to think about reasons. What blood tests were appropriate? This level of gout might even indicate malignancy. He needed to check.

But Ally's face still intruded. He thought about the way she'd reacted to his initial blaze of anger. She'd flinched. A brutal father? His move to reassure her had maybe been appropriate. 'That's dreadful,' he conceded.

'So don't you think you might have acted a bit harshly yourself?' Betty probed. 'Doris said you were mean.'

That was a little unfair. 'I was not mean. She spilled paint over my shoes. They're permanently blue.'

'Like you can't afford to buy new shoes.'

'Most receptionists,' he told her, in a voice laced with warning, 'would be sympathetic to their boss when someone threw blue paint at his expensive shoes.'

She grinned. Betty was sixty years old; she'd been receptionist to the three doctors who'd taken care of Tambrine Creek in living memory; and she knew every single patient's history backward. She was invaluable and she knew it. So she could give as much cheek as she liked.

'I'm more likely to be sympathetic to Ally,' she retorted. 'She needs it. Her grandpa was a harsh man and we worried that her father was worse. I don't think she's had it easy.'

'She shouldn't call herself a doctor.'

'Will you get off your high horse? You know as well as I do that if she puts up a sign saying simply, "Ally Westruther, Massage", every second fisherman's lad will take it the wrong way and she'll be fighting them off with sticks.'

He hadn't thought of that.

'And she's got nothing.' Betty was pushing inexorably on. 'The boys have been helping her set up. She didn't want anyone to help, but this bad weather has everyone bored and they're more than keen to help. So they've insisted. Her room downstairs looks nice now. They've painted it and she has a lovely massage table and a big heater and everything you'd want. But Russ Ewing blew a fuse when he was sandblasting her front steps and he had to go upstairs to change it. She hasn't invited anyone up there and now we know why. She's sleeping on a mattress on the floor. She's got nothing.'

Mrs Skye's medical record was getting less and less attention. Darcy was trying hard to concentrate but it wasn't working. 'Maybe her furniture's coming later.'

'Maybe it's not. Maybe she's broke.'

'She's an adult. If she's been working...'

'Oh, leave it alone.' Betty shook her head, as if in wonder that he could be so obtuse. 'She's a lovely girl, our Ally, and we're going to support her every way can. And we think you should, too. Why don't you recommend that Elsie Skye could use a little rub instead of worrying herself sick about her gout?'

'She doesn't need a massage.'

'Elsie can afford it, she's bored and she's in pain. Have you wondered why her gout flares up so much more when her daughter's in America? I bet our Ally could make her feel lovely.'

'You don't massage gout,' he said stubbornly, and she raised her eyebrows as if he was being thick.

'It's only her feet that have gout. Not all of her. And as if Ally wouldn't know not to massage something that would hurt. She's a doctor!'

'She's not a doctor of medicine.'

'How do you know?'

Darcy set Elsie's history down on the desk with a slap. He was already running late for afternoon surgery and now he was going to be later—because he was gossiping about someone he had no interest in. 'Because if she was a doctor of medicine we'd have that wall knocked out between the buildings in two minutes flat,' he snapped. 'And she'd be in here, with a queue of patients stretched almost out the door waiting to see her. As I have. Now, can we get on with it?'

'Yes, Doctor. Certainly, Doctor,' Betty said with a mock-serious curtsy. 'Only will you just think about it?'

'Will I be allowed not to?'

Her first paying customer.

Treating Gloria Kerr was pure pleasure. She'd walked in and peered around Ally's newly painted rooms and gasped with delight.

'Ooh, love, you have it really nice. Doris said it looked a picture and then she said why didn't I get myself down here? I've been gardening for a week— the oxalis has taken over the lawn and I hate using that weedkiller stuff. I reckon it gets into the ground water. But my back...it's killing me. If you could just give it a nice rub?'

Ally hadn't planned on opening until tomorrow. Her grand opening—i.e. unlocking the front door and hoping someone came—was timed for nine a.m. She didn't have the room exactly as she wanted it. But Gloria looked at her with eyes that were big with hope; and Ally had exactly sixty-five cents left in her purse and she really fancied dinner.

So she chatted to Gloria as she warmed the towels, and then asked Gloria to choose her preferred oils. She chose sandalwood for relaxation. Then she spent an hour giving the lady the best rub she knew how to administer.

She was carefully gentle. Gloria was in her late sixties. She had knots of osteoarthritis, where massage could inflame a joint and cause more problems. She had deep varicose veins that had to be avoided. But Ally's hands moved skilfully, patiently, carefully kneading knotted muscles and easing an aching neck and tired, workworn hands.

'Your fingers are wonderful,' Gloria whispered as finally Ally lay warm towels back over Gloria's body, rested her hands on her back for a moment as a final, lingering contact and then stood back from the table. 'Magic. Oh, my dear, my hands are so warm and soft. You make me feel amazing.'

Part of it was the contact, Ally thought. Gloria Kerr was Doris's sister. Gloria's husband had died just before Ally had left town. Her only son, Bill, was a rough-diamond fisherman who maybe gave his mum a peck on the cheek for Mother's Day and for her birthday. If she was lucky. That was the only human touch she was likely to get.

Massage wasn't a substitute for loving human contact, Ally thought, but it certainly helped. She'd warmed and mobilised Gloria's aching joints. She'd given her time out from her loneliness and she'd listened as Gloria had filled her in on the last seventeen years of town life.

Gloria was happy. She'd sleep much easier tonight because of her massage, and Ally accepted her fee knowing she'd given good service.

It was a start, she thought with satisfaction as she stood on the doorstep and watched Gloria walk off happily down the street. She'd helped.

And best of all she'd been paid. She could eat!

'You know that Gloria has arthritis?'

She whirled to find Darcy Rochester watching her from the front step of his rooms. He looked as if he was about to go out on a house call. Every inch the doctor, he was carrying a smart black doctor's bag and he was headed in the direction of his capacious Mercedes Benz parked out on the street.

A brand-new Mercedes, she thought bitterly. As opposed to her ancient rust-bucket of a panel van which looked almost ludicrous beside it.

'Do you have to keep scaring me?' Ally demanded, and he raised an eyebrow as if such a notion was ludicrous.

'What, you don't have a spare bucket of paint to throw at me this time?'

'I wish,' she muttered darkly. 'And, yes, I do know Gloria has arthritis.'

'So maybe massage isn't appropriate.'

'Go teach your grandmother to suck eggs.'

'I beg your pardon?'

'You know your business and I know mine,' she said through gritted teeth. She was almost deliriously happy to be here again—in this town, setting up her own business—but this man was threatening to burst her fragile bubble of contentment. 'I know what I'm about,' she said, trying to moderate her voice a little. 'I understand that massaging inflammatory joints can cause damage, and I was extremely careful not to do anything of the kind. I helped.'

'She's on medication. If you've interfered—'

What was it with this man?

'I did not,' she said, again through gritted teeth, 'interfere with Gloria's medication in any way, shape or form. I did not imply that she'd be better off taking wart of hog, collected at midnight from the local cemetery in ritualistic sacrifice, than she is taking your boring old anti-inflammatories. I did take a medical history—I'd be stupid not to—but she's your patient, and aside from rubbing her down with a little sandalwood oil...'

'Sandalwood's expensive.'

'So's a Mercedes,' she snapped. 'I charge to cover my expenses. The sandalwood costs me maybe a dollar. I factor it into my accounts. How much do you charge to cover the cost of running your Mercedes?'

Yikes. That was way out of line. She couldn't believe she'd just said it. She wasn't normally this rude—this abrupt. What was it about this man that got under her skin?

But he stood on the doorstep of the place where her grandpa used to practise medicine, and his eyes condemned her.

'Um…we seem to be getting off on the wrong foot,' he said, and she blinked.

'We do indeed.'

'I'm sure you're a fine massage therapist.'

'And I'm sure you're a fine doctor.' Her tone was wary.

'If you'd just like to talk to me about my patients before you treat them.'

'And your patients would be…who? The whole town?'

'I guess.'

'You'd like me to ask permission to touch anyone who comes near me?'

'There's no need to be dramatic.'

'There's every need to be dramatic.' She was practically snarling. 'I'm a massage therapist. Not a witchdoctor. The first rule of a good massage therapist is exactly the same rule as for a good doctor. Do no harm. So, if you'll excuse me, would you just get into your fancy car and take yourself off to wherever you're going? Because I have things to do.'

She certainly did. She had a steak to buy. A really big steak. Gloria's money was practically cooking itself in her pocket.

But Darcy was staring at her as if she'd just arrived from outer space.

'What?' she said crossly.

'I just thought...'

'What?'

'Look, maybe we should get to know each other a little better.'

'I don't think so.'

'It's a small town. I gather you're intending to stay.'

'You're the Johnny-come-lately,' she agreed. 'I'm the local. Maybe you'll move on.'

'It's unlikely.'

'Why not?'

'I like it here.'

'A big fish in a small pond,' she said cordially, and watched the frown snap down.

'Look...'

Maybe she ought to change the subject. She had
no idea why they just had to look at each other
and they started snapping. Conciliation was her
middle name, she thought ruefully, and she had no
idea why this man had the capacity to knock her
right out of her normal pacifist nature.

But she sort of enjoyed it, though, she decided.
Astonishingly. Somehow tossing paint at him at
their first meeting had set her free to bounce insults
around.

Or maybe it had been that when he'd flared in
anger and she'd retreated in fear, he'd made it absolutely clear there'd be no consequences.

Argument for argument's sake was a novel concept, but she was discovering she could enjoy it.
But she did need to move on.

'Did you get your shoes clean?' she queried.

'No,' he said shortly. 'I didn't.'

Honestly, he was irresistible. He stood on the
top step all dressed up like a very important doctor,
and he was so looking like a bubble that had to be
burst.

'You couldn't have tried hard enough,' she told
him, and watched the grey eyes widen in astonishment. He wasn't used to be being teased.

'I got the pavement clean,' she continued,
watching the amazing wash of expressions on his
face. 'I scrubbed and scrubbed and there's not a

trace of blue paint left. So I can be quite useful. There are also times when I don't do harm.'

'I didn't imply…'

'Yes, you did.'

He glowered. And then he glanced at his watch and he glowered some more, while she watched with interest. She had no idea why she was goading this man, but she couldn't stop to save herself.

'We need to talk,' he said at last.

'Why?'

'We just do.' His frown faded and suddenly he was looking at her with an expression that was almost a plea. 'There are problems. Things you should know about.'

'About every patient in town?'

'Of course not,' he conceded. 'But some. If you've got time…'

'I need my dinner.'

He glanced at his watch again. 'It's only five o'clock.'

Yeah, but she hadn't had lunch. And she had enough for a steak.

'Tell you what,' he said. 'I haven't had lunch…'

Snap!

'I'm about to grab a sandwich from the general store. Have you ever had chickenpox?'

What sort of question was that? 'No.'

'Damn.'

'I'm inoculated, though.'

'You're inoculated?' Once again there was a trace of confusion. 'Aren't you too old to have been inoculated?'

'Sorry?'

'Chickenpox inoculation for kids didn't come through until fifteen years back.'

'I had it later, as an adult.' All non-protected doctors did. But what business was it of his?

'Oh.' He was looking at her as if she were some sort of puzzle—a puzzle that had a hundred pieces and he was far too busy to put them together. 'Well, good.'

'Why?'

'I was going to say that I'll buy you a sandwich to keep the wolf from the door, and then take you out to the hills above the town.'

'Are you propositioning me?'

There was a sharp intake of breath on that one. 'Are you listening?' he demanded, and she stifled a giggle. Propositioning her? Maybe not. Did this man know that she was even a woman?

'I'm listening.' She put on her demure tone and received a suspicious glance for her pains.

'I have three really sick kids up in the alternative lifestyle settlement above town,' he told her. 'It's a commune of sorts. They've been hit with chickenpox and I can't bring the really sick ones down to hospital as I'd like. They won't let me.' Then, as she still looked confused, he explained a bit more. 'I have another half-dozen house calls to do before I call it a day, so I don't have time to talk to you about the problems you might be facing, but I do need to talk to you. It's a fifteen-minute drive. Come with me and talk on the way?'

She stared at him. She stared at the big Mercedes.

She looked down at herself.

She'd been painting when Gloria had arrived. She'd put clean jeans and a T-shirt on to do the massage but they weren't exactly the sort of gear this man would expect in any woman he dated.

And their date was with chickenpox?

Plus a sandwich. A free sandwich. And a ride in a very nice car.

'OK, then,' she said, trying hard to sound demure and compliant and not truly excited about a free sandwich. 'I can do that.' She glanced at her watch. 'I have time between clients.'

'When's your next client due?'

'That's for me to know and you to find out,' she told him. 'Can I have my sandwich toasted?'

Which was how, fifteen minutes later, they were heading north out of town, with Ally wrapping herself around a double round of toasted ham, cheese and tomato sandwiches with double the usual cheese and very thick bread.

Darcy had ordered himself a single round of salad sandwiches—how boring was that? He finished them off while he drove, then concentrated on driving with the occasional sideways glance at her.

She'd added a chocolate thick-shake as a side order. It tasted unbelievably wonderful.

'Do you have worms?' he asked, and she almost choked. But didn't. That would be a waste of sandwich and there was no way she was wasting a crumb.

'Why would I have worms?' she demanded with her mouth full, and then added a polite, 'Doctor?'

'I've never met anyone so skinny who eats like you do.'

'Then you haven't lived,' she told him, and turned her attention to her thick-shake again. Some things required full attention.

'So you live on your nerves?'

She sighed. She slurped the rest of her thick-shake and thought about licking the rim. She sighed again, this time in real regret, and let it go. A girl had some standards.

'I don't live on my nerves.'

'So you're bulimic?'

'Right. A bulimic call-girl.'

'Hey…'

'Do we have to get so personal?' she asked him.

'I just want to know.'

'Well, I don't particularly want to tell. No, I am not bulimic, Dr Rochester. I'm disgustingly healthy. So set your professional concerns aside and tell me why you're bringing me on this drive to see chickenpoxes. I assume you don't think they want a massage?'

'No, I—'

'Good. Rubbing poxes would make them itch.'

'You know—'

'Just tell me what you want me to hear.'

He hesitated. She waited. This car was really lovely, she thought. It must have cost him a bomb. If she set up her own medical plate in the main street of somewhere like Tambrine Creek, then maybe…

Yeah, right.

'Tell me,' she said again, and this time there was an edge of anger in her voice that she didn't try and disguise.

'There are some vulnerable people in this town.'

'Really?'

'Really,' he said angrily. 'Will you just listen? You haven't been near this place for nearly twenty years.'

'So you think I'm about to prey on the population.'

'I bought you a sandwich,' he snapped. 'Listen.'

'Fine,' she said. She set her empty shake container in the cute little drink holder between the seats, folded her hands in her lap and stared straight ahead. 'In payment for my sandwich I'll be quiet. But only because you let me have double cheese.' Her voice became totally subservient. 'Please, sir, I'm paying attention. You can start now.'

Silence. Then a sound from the driver's side that might almost be…a chuckle?

She ventured a suspicious glance at him and found his lips were twitching. And those eyes…

Laughter did something to him, she thought, and tried very hard to stay looking demure and compliant and good.

'OK.' He took a visible hold on his sudden and unexpected flicker of humour, and gripped the steering wheel harder. 'There are a few people I need to talk about.'

'I'm listening.'

'Ivy Morrison,' he said, and there was a touch of desperation in his voice that said that laughter wasn't too far away.

'What about Ivy Morrison?'

'She's on a pension.' Laughter faded. 'She's a little simple. She buys every new thing that's going and gets into the most appalling financial mess. She'll be desperate to see you.'

'I'll see her.'

'Are you listening?' he demanded. 'She can't afford you.'

'So you're saying I should say, ''Sorry, Ivy, the doctor says you're too poor to see me''?'

'No, I—'

'Because that would be insulting and humiliating,' she told him.

'Yeah, but—'

'What I can do is take her the first time. I'll only accept cash—which I do anyway as I can't afford credit facilities—and I'll tell her that frequent massage isn't indicated in someone really fit and healthy. I'll also make sure that the only appointments I have available for her are on the day before pension day. Never the day after. OK?'

There was a silence. Then he said, 'You understand about pension days?'

'Of course I do.' Did she ever. She knew all about eating reasonably in the first days after you received it and starving in the days before it arrived.

But this was no time for reminiscences. Darcy was still watching her curiously.

'You'd do that for Ivy?'

'Of course. I'd do it for anyone I thought needed that level of care. This is my home and this is my community. I'm not about to exploit it.'

'You really feel like that about Tambrine Creek?'

'It's the only home I've ever known,' she told him. 'I'm not about to mess things up by being greedy.'

'I don't suppose you are.' His voice fell away. He was clearly unsure where she was coming from.

As she was.

'What about you?' she asked, moving on. 'You've told me you have a very romantic mother and you have a wood stove. What else?'

'Sorry?'

'What's the rest of the story?'

'I don't know what you mean.'

'You're not married? Gloria says you share the doctor's house with two dogs and a bunch of chooks.'

'Easier than a wife and kids,' he said with mock seriousness, and she grinned.

'I guess. OK. Why are you in Tambrine Creek?'

'I like it.'

'Most med students could think of nothing worse than heading straight to Tambrine Creek when there are heaps of jobs available in the cities. Gloria said you just arrived here five years ago to practise and you've never made any attempt to leave.'

'I told you—I like it.'

'But there must be a reason why you came.'

'What's the phrase you used?' he demanded. 'That's for me to know and you to find out?'

But he wasn't laughing. Ally looked at his hands on the steering wheel and saw his knuckles were white. There was a story here.

Yeah, well, that makes two of us, she thought wryly. Two of them running from ghosts.

There was no time for more. 'Here we are.' He was steering the big car along a dirt track leading from the ridge overlooking the town.

'They live here?' she asked incredulously, and he nodded.

'They do.'

'This belongs to Gareth Hatfield. Or it did.'

'Gareth Hatfield? I've never heard of him.'

'He's…um… His son was a…a friend of my father's,' she said, her voice trailing off. Then, realising something more was expected, she tried again. 'The old man was filthy rich. He bought all the land around here and then sold it off for a vast profit. The locals used to say he'd find some sucker to sell even this place to, and maybe he has. Is there water up here now?' Tambrine Creek itself was set on a rich coastal plain, but the land up here was rough and rock-strewn. It was so dry it was almost dust.

'They cart their water up from the river,' Darcy told her.

She fell silent, staring about her. She could see three rough bush huts set well back into the scrub. The place seemed deserted. The huts were primitive and there were no vehicles parked where the track ended.

'No one's here.'

'They'll be inside. Between five and six o'clock, the women cook and the men meditate.'

She swallowed. Memories came flooding back. To have such a community here...now... But Darcy was still watching her, waiting for a reaction. She could see she was starting to puzzle him. What had he said? The women cook. 'Lucky women.'

'You'd rather cook than meditate?' he asked, and she struggled to make her voice sound normal.

'Of course I would. I'd rather cook than do anything. Especially when I get to eat what I cook. Where are the cars?'

'There aren't cars. They don't believe in them.'

'How do they get water up here?'

'The women carry it.'

Her jaw dropped. 'You're kidding. It's a half-mile climb.'

'Yeah.'

'Meditation's looking good,' she whispered. She'd thought, when Jerome had left the country, that such communities were a thing of the past. But maybe it was a lifestyle attractive for a lot of people.

It still horrified her. 'I'm feeling a really strong bout of feminism coming on,' she managed.

'Try and keep it to yourself,' he advised. He pulled the car to a halt and reached into the back for his bag. 'Value judgements aren't wanted here.'

'Then what are you doing here?' she demanded, shaking her sense of unreality and trying to haul herself back to the present. 'You, the very king of value judgements.'

'What do you mean?'

'A greedy, money-sucking, bulimic call-girl.'

'OK.' He held up his hands in surrender. 'OK. Enough. Truce. You want to come inside or stay in the car?'

'You'd trust me with real people?' Then, at his look, she suddenly relented. 'I may as well. I guess I could hike off home—if the women cart water up here it seems a bit soppy to whinge about a hike of an hour or so—but...'

'There are still people I want to talk to you about.'

'More Ivys? More people you don't trust me with?'

'Ally...'

She sighed. 'Oh, goody. It seems I'm going to be insulted all the way home again, too. OK. I'll stay. I might have to find someone here I can insult in turn.'

'Please.'

'I know.' She shrugged but then she smiled again. 'Not appropriate. You don't need to worry. I'll be good. You'll hear no value judgements from me. I won't charge anyone for massage. I'll do no harm. It was a truly excellent thick-shake and they were wonderful sandwiches, Dr Rochester. They were even worth being good for.'

CHAPTER THREE

THE hut they entered was a shock.

She'd forgotten how appalling it could be. Ally walked through the door and the first thing that hit her was the smell.

Smells. Plural.

There were pigs hanging round the yard, and a pile of dung by the door was attracting flies, inside and out. Smoke permeated the room, with the vague smell of hundreds of past meals—not all of them appetising. And human smells.

There was a lot to be said for deodorant, Ally thought grimly as the stench reached out to hit her. Then she amended the thought. No. There was a lot to be said for washing.

The smell was overpowering. And the sensation that the past was closing in on her.

Unaware of the vast wash of remembrance flooding over his companion, Darcy didn't pause. Clearly he'd been here before. He didn't knock— there was no door, just a gap in the timber slabs that made the wall.

'How are they?' he asked before Ally even had time to get used to the gloom. There was a fire smouldering in the centre of the hut, and smoke was wisping up toward a rough hole in the centre of the roof. Not all of it was escaping.

It looked like something out of the Stone Age, Ally thought, and had to swallow and swallow again as she fought for control. It was just like…just like…

A figure emerged from the gloom, a woman, skirt to the floor, hair braided down her back, dirty and…a little bit desperate? She'd been sitting on one of the benches that ran around the walls, and from under a bundle of blankets came a thin, despairing cry.

A sick child? It was a little girl, Ally decided as her eyes adjusted to the smoke-filled room. The child looked about six or seven. Her face was colourless and her sandy curls were a tangled mat on the hessian sack that served as a pillow.

The woman didn't greet Darcy. She didn't look at him. She stood, her shoulders slumped in a stance of absolute despair, and she stared at the floor. 'Jody's worse,' she whispered.

Dear heaven. Ally was almost overwhelmed with disbelief. That this could be happening again…

Darcy was already kneeling by the child. He motioned back toward Ally. 'This is Ally Westruther,' he said briefly. 'A friend.'

The woman lifted her head for a moment to glance apathetically at Ally, and then she stared at the floor again.

'I can't make her eat anything.'

'Is she drinking?'

'A little.'

'Have you been doing the fluid chart?'

'Yes.' She pulled a tatty piece of paper from her pocket and Darcy studied it with concern.

'Hell, Margaret, she's not even close to even fluid balance.' He lifted the little girl's wrist, but even from where she was Ally could guess that the pulse would be weak and thready. Sick kids—really sick kids—weren't the ones that came into Emergency, crying. They were silent and limp and scary.

'How long's she been like this?' she asked, and the woman cast her a distracted glance.

'Three days now. The other two are a bit better.'

'That's something.' Darcy was putting a thermometer under the little girl's armpit. 'You mean they're eating and drinking again.'

'Yes. But Marigold's arm looks really red— she's been scratching so much we can't stop it getting infected. She says it hurts under her arm as well, and in her neck.'

'Hell, you need to let me give antibiotics.'

'He won't let us.'

Darcy sat back on his heels. He waited in silence until the thermometer had had time to register.

A chicken wandered in the open door and started to scratch in the dust around the fire.

He lifted the thermometer free and winced.

'It's high, isn't it?' the woman said, as if it was a foregone conclusion.

'She's had high temperatures for almost a week. She's not getting any fluid on board. Margaret, she must come to hospital.'

'No. He won't—'

'He has to let her come. She needs an intravenous drip to get fluids on board. She needs antibiotics.'

'Give her fluids here.'

'You know I can't. Margaret, look around. There are reasons the kids' sores are infected.'

'I can't help it. We do our best.'

'I need to see Jerry.'

'He won't—'

'Jerry?' Ally froze.

'Jerry's the head of the community.' Darcy was totally occupied with the child but he talked to her over his shoulder. 'There are three women and four men here, but Jerry's the head.'

'We do as he says,' Margaret whispered.

'Even if it means someone dies?' Darcy demanded, and the woman gasped. He hadn't referred to Jody by name but his meaning was un-mistakable.

'No.'

'It may well happen.'

'No!'

'Then let Jody go to hospital. You're her mother.'

'Jerry says no. You know he says no.'

'I'll have to bring in Social Services.'

'You know he won't let them take her. Last time he went into the bush and stayed there. You know what happened then. And even if you report it…' Her voice broke on a sob. 'It takes weeks for them to do anything, and when they come he's so reasonable and he makes them feel like everything's under control.'

'It isn't though, is it, Margaret?'

'N-no,' she faltered. 'But I'm only one. I can't… The group decides.'

'Lorraine's Marigold is sick, too, and she's just as upset.'

'Lorraine won't fight Jerry. Neither will Penny, and David's sick, too.'

'You must. You all must.' But Darcy's voice was weary, as if he'd had this argument a thousand times before.

But Ally was no longer listening.

She stared down at the sick little girl and she felt like she might explode.

Jerry. Jerome. Jerome was here?

'Where's Jerry?' Ally asked—casually, but her voice was loaded. This whole situation… She might choke, she thought. After all these years.

'He's meditating,' Margaret told her. 'The men are. Penny and Lorraine are making dinner in the other hut.'

'The other kids are there?' Darcy demanded.

'Yes.'

'I'll see them.' Darcy rose. 'But when I leave I'm taking Jody with me, Margaret.'

'You can't.'

'If I don't…' He glanced down at the little girl who was staring up at him with eyes that didn't seem to be registering. 'You know what will happen. It's happened before.'

'Sam was an accident.'

'A burn that got infected. That I wasn't allowed to treat.'

Ally stepped back and gripped one of the wall supports, leaning heavily against it. The room was spinning. She felt sick. Jerome Hatfield. It had to be him. In this place, after all these years.

And a little boy called Sam had died of burns. Dear God, how much more damage had he done?

'He's in the far hut?' she demanded, and the woman looked at her, startled. The fury in her voice was unmistakable.

'Yes.'

'I'll talk to him,' she said, and wheeled.

Darcy caught her before she reached the door. He'd moved like lightning, reaching her to grip her arm and stop her from going further.

'Leave it,' he said roughly. 'I'll see him.'

'Yeah, like you've done a lot so far.' She was so angry she didn't care who heard her fury. 'A little boy dead? And now Jody. I don't believe this. Let me go.'

'You'll do more harm than good,' he said urgently. 'If you threaten him he'll take himself off to the bush and take his people with him. He's done it in the past. When Sam died.'

'And you let it happen?'

'I didn't have a choice,' he told her. 'They watch the road. When Sam was ill I was so desperate I even called in the police. But they couldn't find them. And now… It's taken me ages to persuade Jerry to let me come and treat the kids.'

'But you let the children stay.'

'There's been a Social Services hearing,' he told her, and she could hear years of frustration in his voice. 'Margaret loves her kids. Social Services knows that. So do Lorraine and Penny. Jerry's agreed to let the kids be assessed once a month. Hell, Ally.'

Enough. His hands were tied. She could see that. Focus on Jody. Focus on one child's needs.

Margaret loved her little girl, she thought, watching the woman's face. But…did she love Jerry more?

Who could possibly love Jerry?

'Margaret, you can't possibly want to stay with Jerry when it's putting Jody in danger.' She hesitated and moved to face her. She reached out and gripped her shoulders, forcing her to meet her eyes. 'You can't.'

'You don't know what he's like,' Margaret whispered. 'I'm his. We're all his. When Sam died, Penny tried to leave but…she came back. He'd find us.'

'So you're scared of him?'

'Of course we are.'

'There's no physical abuse,' Darcy said from behind her. 'We went through that after Sam died. Margaret might say this now, but if the authorities come in Jerry will have all their support.'

'Right.' She took a deep breath. 'I do know what he's like, Margaret. And I can deal with this. I promise.'

'How the hell?' Darcy was looking at her as if she was out of her mind.

'Bring the rest of the kids and the women here,' she told Margaret. 'Things are going to change. Right now.'

'You'll destroy…' Margaret looked appalled.

'No,' Ally told her. Once upon a time she'd been terrified of Jerry Hatfield herself, but that was going back almost twenty years. No more. And that these women and these kids—probably the men, too—were going through what she'd faced.

'I've waited a long time for this,' she said. 'Trust me. I can cope with Jerry Hatfield. Darcy, give me your phone.'

'What—?'

'I don't have a cell phone,' she told him, as if he were being stupid. 'I need it.' Then, as he didn't react, she stepped forward and lifted it from the clip on his belt.

She started dialling.

And she started walking.

'If you want to see what a massage therapist can do when she decides to do no harm, come along and watch,' she told him over her shoulder. 'But this tragedy will stop right now.' And she started talking urgently into Darcy's cell phone.

He followed. He hardly had a choice.

Whatever harm she did…well, it couldn't be worse than what was happening, he thought. His intention now was to put Jody into his car and take her down to the hospital, facing the consequences later. There would be consequences. To physically remove a child from her parents…

It didn't matter. It couldn't matter. The alternative was Jody's death, and he wasn't prepared to have what had happened to Sam happen to another child. Sam's death had occurred in the first month he'd been in Tambrine Creek and he still felt dreadful that he hadn't done more. He'd called in the social workers, rather than taking things into his own hands, and it had backfired dreadfully.

But what on earth was Ally about? He watched in stunned amazement as she spoke urgently to someone on the other end of the phone and then stomped furiously across to the neighbouring hut. She was only about five feet one or five feet two. She was slightly built. Her jeans were faded, her shirt had a paint streak down the back and she was wearing flip-flops. Her long blonde hair hung down her back, and it swayed as she walked, accentuating her entire stance of fury.

She looked like David stalking off to face Goliath, he thought, and he quickened his steps to join her.

Should he stop her?

Maybe not, he decided. This situation had reached breaking point. There was no use skirting round the issues at stake, because those issues involved a child's life.

But what did she know about this? He was under no illusion that her anger was solely caused by one sick child, justified as that was. She'd reacted too fast, too directly.

What had she called Jerry? Jerry Hatfield? The name the group's leader was using was Jerry Dwyer.

What did Ally know of him?

All he could do was watch. He arrived at the hut door two seconds after Ally did, and by the time he arrived she was already in action.

This was the meditation hut. He'd glanced in here once, but the women had almost seemed afraid of it. 'We only go in there to clean,' he'd been told.

The two living huts were putrid but this was lighter and brighter, with a ring of bright candles around the perimeter sending a golden glow over a group of four men kneeling on prayer mats in the centre.

But the glow was fading. Ally was kicking every candle over, pushing its wick into the dust.

She was ignoring the men.

'What the…?'

Jerry was the first to rise.

The other three men were spineless. Darcy had decided that early in his encounters with the group. Acolytes who didn't have the courage to stand up to Jerry, they simply did as he said in all things. It was Jerry who called the tune.

Jerry was in his late fifties or early sixties, a huge bull of a man, habitually dressed in a vast purple caftan with his beard and hair falling almost to his waist. He seemed a bit mad, Darcy had decided. His people were afraid of him, and even though there'd been no proven physical abuse, he guessed there was good reason for their fear.

Ally didn't seem afraid of him, though. She kicked over the last candle and then stalked over to face him.

'Jerome Hatfield,' she said in a voice that was rich with loathing. 'I can't believe it's you.'

'I'm Jerry Dwyer.' The man was off balance. He obviously didn't recognise the woman in front of him and he hadn't a clue what was going on.

He hadn't noticed Darcy standing by the entrance, and for the moment Darcy was content to merge into the shadows. And wait.

Maybe he should take the child now while Jerry was distracted, he thought, but then…he could hardly abandon Ally. And Margaret would never let him take her surreptitiously. He intended to take Jody, but he'd have to face Jerry as he did it.

'You're Jerome Hatfied,' Ally was saying. 'Jerry if you like, but it makes no difference. Don't lie to me.'

'I have no idea—'

'You have every idea,' she spat. 'I can't believe you had the nerve to come back here. After all this time. If your father knew…'

'My father has nothing to do with you,' Jerry said, in the great booming voice he used so well to intimidate everyone who came within hearing. 'Get out of my prayer house.'

'I don't know who you're praying to,' Ally told him, lowering her voice to almost a whisper. It was an incredible contrast to Jerry's booming vocal, but it was every bit as effective. Just as menacing. 'But I tell you now. Nobody's listening. Why would anyone listen to your prayers, Jerome Hatfield, when you don't even listen to the people around you? When you let children die.'

'Get out.'

'You know,' she said, suddenly switching her attention to the three men still crouched in disbelief on the prayer mats, 'if I were you guys, I'd get out now. Consorting with a known criminal is an offence all by itself.'

'I'm not—'

'Oh, yes, you are.' She kept the hush to her tone. There was no need to raise her voice. Even the chickens seemed to have stilled to listen. 'You left this country seventeen years ago, while you were on bail for assault, forgery, bigamy, theft…you name it. You left a trail of destruction in your wake, including two wives. The police tracked you down twelve years ago and found you doing the same thing in the States. But you ran again, before you could be deported. I'd hoped we'd seen the last of you then, but suddenly—guess what? A man called Jerry Dwyer is living on a barren bush block that no one ever comes near. It's unsaleable land. Your father owns it and you know he's written it off as unusable. So you come back, pick up another lot of vulnerable people and start all over again.'

'You don't know—'

'Of course I know,' she said wearily. 'Do you think I'm stupid? I'm Ally Westruther but, like you, I've changed my surname. Try Ally Lindford for size.'

'Lindford.'

'That's right,' she said, almost pleasantly. 'Tony Lindford's daughter.'

He stared as if he couldn't believe his eyes. 'Tony's… You're *Ally*?'

'That's right.'

'Tony's dead.'

'Of course he's dead,' she agreed, almost cordially. 'You don't care about that, though, do you? Like you didn't care about my mother and like you didn't care about any of your people. You're a liar and a sham.'

He took a deep breath. Searching for control. 'Get out of my house,' he boomed.

She ignored him. 'This man…' she said, almost conversationally, and Darcy was suddenly aware that there was a cluster of women and children behind him. 'This man sucks people for everything he can get. Don't tell me. Let me guess. This man will have control of all your pension books. You'll all have been on pensions when he met you. That's why he chose you. He'll give you nothing. You'll be half-starving, you'll work like slaves for him and he'll never be pleased. He'll control every aspect of your lives and he'll never let go. Ever.'

'These people want to be here,' Jerry snarled, and Ally gave him a look that would curdle milk.

'These people have been so brainwashed they don't know any better. You prey on desperate people when they're at their weakest. But there is better. There's welfare services where we can get everyone emergency accommodation. There's free medical treatment for the kids.' She motioned down to one of the men and her voice softened. 'As for you, that's a skin cancer on your face. If you don't get it off soon, it'll be so deep that you'll be scarred for life. Even now I'd imagine you must be in dreadful pain. You desperately need a skin graft.'

The man put a hand to the side of his head. The wound looked angry and inflamed—incredibly painful.

'I've told him—' Darcy started, but she cut him off.

'It doesn't matter what you told him,' she said. 'No one can listen. Not when Jerry overrules everything you say. He's blocked their ears. But you all need to listen now.'

'Get out!' The big man was practically screaming, and he made as if to lunge at Ally. Darcy took a step toward her, but she sidestepped neatly—as if she'd done it many times before?—then turned again to face Jerry.

'I was deathly afraid of you,' she told him. 'Once. But I escaped. And now you all can. This man is nothing but a liar and a thief and a con merchant. And if you listen you might be able to hear a car in the distance. It's the police. They're coming, Jerry. I just phoned them. You have outstanding warrants in at least two countries. I've contacted them and told them where you are. They're coming to arrest you right now.'

'I…' He was almost speechless. He whirled to his men. 'Get up. Move!' Then to the women. 'Move, now. Out the back way. We can leave.'

'But I know where all your caves are, Jerry,' Ally told him, almost pleasantly. 'They're a great labyrinth to hide in, but not if the searchers know the way. So you can go where you like and I'll send the police after you. But as for the rest of you…' She softened again and faced them all. 'I know what this man is like,' she told them. 'I can help. Believe me, I can help, and so will Dr Rochester. Your kids are ill. You know that. You're ill yourselves. If you trust us, stay here and let us help. Or trust Jerry as you've trusted him for years and see where that gets you.'

Silence.

'Come on,' Jerry yelled. He swept toward the entrance. There was a pile of firewood in his way and he gave it a vicious kick. A branch swung out and hit Ally's foot—hard—but she appeared not to notice. Darcy started forward instinctively but she held up a hand as if to stop him.

'Let him go,' she told him. She looked at Jerry with contempt. 'It's not worth our while trying to stop him. He won't get far. Not now. It's over.'

Jerry swore.

Ally smiled and moved aside to let him leave. 'Bye, Jerome,' she said softly. 'See you soon.'

He stared at her for a long, speechless moment—and then he was gone, with a sweep of purple cloth and trailing a string of invective after him.

No one moved. Finally one of the men on the floor gave a frightened whimper and scuttled after him.

Nobody else followed.

By the time the first police car turned into the clearing, Jerry and his one faithful acolyte had left on foot, heading into the bushland behind the huts. But the others were clustered around in a terrified huddle, and at the centre of the huddle was Ally.

Darcy couldn't help. He was forced to focus on medical need. Jody needed him desperately. He set up a saline drip within minutes of Jerry leaving. Margaret was too confused to argue and there was no time for further discussion. He worked over Jody as Margaret darted between her daughter's bedside and the group outside.

She was crying, but by the time Darcy was content to leave Jody's bedside she was calming down.

Everyone was calming down.

It seemed Ally was in control.

When he emerged from the hut where Jody lay, Ally was giving the police specific directions as to where Jerry would be—and reasons why they should arrest him when they found him. The reasons made him blink in disbelief. She knew everything about Jerry. Every criminal charge that had ever been made against him. Outstanding warrants. Crimes committed overseas. Everything. And she was intent on throwing the book at him.

'I don't believe you just did that,' he told Ally faintly as she finally fell silent, and Ally grinned in faint embarrassment.

'Massage therapists rock,' she managed. 'Go get a drip into Jody.'

'I've started a drip.'

'There's two more kids to attend to.'

'Thank you, Dr Westruther,' he told her, and her grin widened at the irony in his tone.

'Think nothing of it,' she said kindly. 'Well? What are you waiting for? Off you go. I can handle the rest.'

'Yeah?'

'Are you OK here, Doc?' Sergeant Matheson, a big beefy police sergeant who'd been transferred to Tambrine Creek almost at the same time as Darcy had arrived, was looking from Ally to Darcy with confusion. 'If what Ally says is right then we need to get this guy.'

Darcy looked around at the huddle of confused people. There was fear here and there was urgent medical need, but nothing he couldn't cope with. Nothing. And the thought was suddenly wonderful. Without Jerry's poisonous influence he could help these people, he thought jubilantly. Finally he could do some good.

Thanks to this slip of a girl.

'If I were you I'd assume what Ally says is right,' he told the policeman. 'I have no idea how or why, but suddenly our massage therapist has all the answers.'

The next few hours were filled with pure medical need.

Darcy phoned the hospital and brought up reinforcements. Betty, his receptionist-cum-nursing-sister, arrived first, followed by another local nurse to assist with the kids who were ill. The social worker was hauled away from a conference at the nearest big town, and the supervisor of the marine refuge came, too. Because Tambrine Creek was the southernmost harbour for Tasmanian shipping, the town was set up with a marine refuge—emergency accommodation for sailors who needed to run for cover in foul weather. This wasn't the first time Darcy had used it for family crises.

But he himself had to focus on Jody. Regardless of the chaos, as soon as Betty arrived he had to take the child down to the hospital. She'd been dehydrated for so long. He was desperately worried about her.

He left the settlement, torn by his need to stay, but Ally was moving through the confusion with assurance. She was reassuring, hugging and talking to everyone and generally acting as if she was almost one of them.

'Don't worry about me getting back to town,' she told him as he lifted Jody into the back of his car and helped Margaret in after her. 'I'll get a lift with the police when I'm ready.'

'The police won't leave until they find Jerry.' The police sergeant had called in reinforcements and there were half a dozen officers treking through the bush now.

'That's right,' Ally said in quiet satisfaction. 'They won't. But neither will I. I've given them directions where to go, and I intend to wait here until he's arrested. Even if I have to go in and hunt myself.'

She smiled.

Why the smile? There were so many unanswered questions, but there was no time to ask them. He had to go.

Betty followed him to the hospital an hour later, bringing the other two children he'd been concerned about. Four-year-old Marigold had a suppurating wound on her arm, with the nodes in her neck and armpit affected. David, aged seven, was running a temperature that had Betty worried. Surprisingly, the kids came without their mothers.

'Ally's organising Penny and Lorraine and the rest of the kids into the refuge,' Betty told him. 'But she persuaded Lorraine and Penny that you and I would look after these two.' She smiled. 'You should have heard the nice things she said about you as a doctor. It'd make you blush. Especially after all those rotten things you said about her.'

'Enough,' Darcy growled. Hell, she knew how to make a man feel bad. 'Let's get these kids seen to.'

Surprisingly, the kids were compliant and almost cheerful as they were washed and fed and tucked into bed. There was nothing wrong with them that fluids and a good dose of antibiotics wouldn't clear up, Darcy thought in satisfaction as he watched Marigold drift into sleep. The kids were supervised now by a nurse who looked as pleased by the outcome of the afternoon's events as Darcy felt. It was little wonder. The whole township had been disturbed by the group living up on the ridge but until now there had been nothing anyone had been able to do about it. Until now.

Until Ally.

As they cleaned up, Betty told him what had happened.

'Ally gave the police directions to the caves and they found him almost straightaway,' she told him. 'And while I was there, Sergeant Matheson got confirmation of what Ally had told him. It was radioed through from the city. Ally's right. There are outstanding warrants everywhere.'

'Why didn't we know?'

'No one knew it was him. I knew Jerome Hatfield when he was a child, but I've never heard of him since he was fifteen or sixteen. No one knew about the caves either. Apparently even the women didn't know the caves were there. I've never heard of them.'

Betty had been raised here in Tambrine Creek. She knew everything that happened to everyone.

'Then how did Ally know all this?'

'Don't ask me,' she told him. 'But we have three kids safe in the kids' ward. How good is that? Is Margaret still here?'

'We offered her a hot shower before we put her to bed next to Jody,' Darcy told her. 'She stood under the shower like she'd never felt hot water before. When she got out, the nurses said she almost toppled over, and she was asleep as soon as her head hit the pillows. She's been desperately worried about Jody for so long. Now they're both dead to the world. Jody's drip is running well, and her colour's starting to improve already.'

'They're all dreadfully emaciated,' Betty said seriously. 'It's no wonder the chickenpox hit hard.'

'The rest are at the refuge?' Darcy asked.

'Yeah. Ally's with them now.'

'Ally…'

'She helped me assess the kids,' Betty told him. 'She's really good.'

'I thought the social worker was helping.'

'Elsa's fine at what she does,' Betty said diffidently. 'But as for helping holding a kid down while I check his temperature…'

'You had to do that?'

'Marigold tried to bite me,' she said ruefully. 'They're like wild kittens. But Ally was terrific.'

He looked down at the two children lying in bed like two little angels. Marigold had drifted to sleep, her little body exhausted by infection, but David was watching them with eyes that practically enveloped his face.

Wild kittens? Scared maybe, but not wild.

'It's OK,' Darcy told him, giving him a reassuring smile. 'You know that, don't you, mate? Your mother's being looked after and you'll see her in the morning.'

David nodded, as if this had already been discussed. 'Ally said she was going to make Mum have a hot shower and toasted sandwiches. And Ally said that if I came here with Betty, and let you wash me and put me to bed and look after me, then I'd be able to have toasted sandwiches whenever I want. And she said you could get me something called a thick-shake that's chocolate but you drink it. She said you were a doctor who gave people the best thick-shakes ever.'

How to make a wild kitten compliant? Chocolate thick-shakes. Of course. Why hadn't he thought of that? 'Betty, can we get the kid a thick-shake?' Darcy asked in a voice that was none too steady. 'And maybe another one in case Marigold wakes up in the night. It seems she's been promised one, too.'

'Thick-shakes?'

'From Beryl's general store,' he told her. 'Tell Beryl to make it just like the one she made for Ally.'

'OK,' Betty said, with a curious look at her boss. 'If you say so.'

'I didn't say so,' he said ruefully. 'Ally said so.' He gave David a grin and then turned to the next need. The next medical imperative.

'I still have house calls to make,' he told her. Damn, he wanted to go to the refuge, but he had conflicting needs. 'I can put most of them off but not Mrs Lewis.'

Marilyn Lewis lived alone and he was worried about her. She'd had two minor heart attacks before this. By rights she should have had bypass surgery two years ago but she refused to consider it. Because she was terrified. But heart pain by itself was enough to terrify her. Now he'd promised he'd call. She'd be desperately worried about herself and if he didn't make it there tonight, maybe she'd even be terrified enough to bring on another attack.

'Maybe I can get someone to check,' Betty said doubtfully. 'But...'

'I know. With four extra patients we don't have spare staff. I need to go myself.'

'But you should check the refuge. Ally said you'd come in and tell the other two mothers how these two are. And the guy with the sore face... Ally told him you'd talk to him about it tonight.'

'She takes a lot on herself,' he snapped, and she nodded. Thoughtfully.

'She does.' She ventured a wry smile. 'I guess she had no right getting Jerry arrested like that.'

'I didn't mean—'

'I know you didn't,' she said cheerfully. 'But I guess if we're pleased she's done that, then we'd better go along with the rest. There's no need to rush to the refuge straightaway. She has things under control.'

'How can she possibly have things under control?' he demanded, suddenly so exasperated he couldn't believe it. 'We don't even know who Ally Westruther is.'

'She's Dr Westruther's grandkid. Of course we know who she is.'

'She says she's a Dr Westruther herself.'

'Well, you know, I wouldn't be the least surprised if she turned out to be just that,' Betty said thoughtfully. 'She handled the kids like a professional.'

'Yeah, a professional masseuse.'

'Get off your high horse,' she advised him kindly. 'She's doing a fine job, whatever her qualifications. You just do what you have to do, and trust that Ally will have things under control. She's quite a lady.'

'Yeah. Right.'

He did go and see Marilyn Lewis. With Betty's assurance that things at the refuge were under control, he adjusted his priorities, but there was still Marilyn. Damn the woman, why wouldn't she agree to a bypass? Her neighbour had rung Darcy earlier to say she was looking distressed. Darcy had rung her and offered to send the ambulance, but Marilyn had refused.

'There's no way I'm going to hospital. It's just a little chest pain and I'm used to chest pain. There's always chest pain.'

'Janet says you're sweating.'

'It's warm.'

'Marilyn...'

'I'm fine,' she'd told him. 'If you'd care to drop in after work and have a cup of tea, you'd be very welcome, but there's no need to fuss.'

There was a need for fuss. If Jody's need up on the ridge hadn't been even more urgent, he would have seen her hours ago.

She'd have to go to hospital, he thought grimly, and spent his time on the road trying to figure out how to persuade her.

There was no persuasion necessary. When Marilyn finally admitted him into the house he discovered that she'd spent her waiting time packing her suitcase.

'I thought you'd never get here,' she told him. She was little and fussy and prim, dressed in a bright pink dressing-gown and pale blue slippers, and her Marilyn Monroe hairstyle looked just a little ridiculous on someone well into her sixties. 'I could have died,' she said in some indignation.

He eyed her with caution. 'Are you thinking of dying?'

'I have really bad chest pains.'

'Can I listen to your heart?'

'When you get me to hospital.'

He thought about that and decided it was worth pushing for the next level. 'Can I send you straight to Melbourne for a bypass?'

'Of course not,' she said in some indignation. 'Don't be foolish. But tell me all the news. You've had such an exciting afternoon. It's all over town. I knew there was something wrong with those people. I knew it. And now I hear you have those three little kiddies in hospital and one of their mothers, too. And one of the men has such a wound on his face. He'll be in there soon, too, I expect.'

The suitcase was thus explained, and Darcy had to fight to stop himself from breaking into a chuckle. Marilyn might be terrified of medical intervention, but her priority was to be where the action was. Her previous visits to hospital had been boring affairs when there'd been no interesting fellow patients. But now...if she was admitted she'd be in the middle of *news*.

Still, there was no doubting that she was frightened about her chest pain, Darcy thought, watching her wince a little as she talked. He stopped her from heaving the suitcase off her bed, and made her sit while he listened to her chest and took her blood pressure. It was erratic enough for him to think maybe the excitement of the afternoon had been a blessing. She needed to be admitted, and if that was what it took…

'OK. A couple of days' bed rest while we get the angina under control will suit you fine,' he told her. 'Dr Harper will be here on Thursday and I'll get him to see you.' Ross Harper was a visiting cardiologist and he'd treated Marilyn before.

'That will be very nice, dear,' Marilyn said serenely. 'And do you know what else I want to do while I'm in your hospital?'

'What?'

'I want to have a nice little massage. I've heard our Ally is wonderful. Do you think she'd do hospital visits?'

He practically choked. Massage visits…

'I can't see why she wouldn't,' Marilyn added, serenely confident that her plan would go ahead. 'Can you?'

'Um…' Think of a reason, he told himself desperately. 'I haven't had her professional qualifications checked.'

'Do you think she's a liar?' Marilyn sounded shocked, and he had to bite his tongue.

'No,' he said shortly as he helped her into his car. 'I don't.' There was silence for a bit as he drove but he was sure Marilyn had been a glorious gossip all her life. Maybe…

'Do you know someone called Gareth Hatfield?' he asked her.

'Oh, no, dear.' Marilyn nestled back on the sumptuous leather and sighed with pleasure. One of the reasons he'd bought this car had been that his patients loved it. Sure, there was an ambulance for transporting patients but it was an ancient battered truck. If possible, most of his patients elected to use Darcy's free Mercedes service.

Did she know Gareth Hatfield?

'Not any more,' she told him.

'But you did once?'

'He was a few years older than I was. Not a very nice man, dear. He owned so much land around here and he made such a profit selling it to those who'd leased it from him for years and years. No. Not a nice man. He never lived here—he just used to come and harass people into paying more than they could afford. And then that boy of his...he was a bad lot.'

'Jerry?'

'Jerome. He lived with his mother, and as far as I know he hardly ever came here, but when he did—ooh, he was a nasty little boy. His father used to come to check on his properties, and while he and the bank manager discussed how much they could make from the locals, Jerome would swagger round as if he owned the place. I seem to remember he and Ally's father were friends for a while—or Jerry ordered and Tony followed—but that came to nothing. They were worlds apart.'

Friends? Jerry and Ally's father had been friends?

There were so many unanswered questions.

But there was no time to think of the answers. For the next thirty minutes Darcy had to force himself to concentrate purely on medicine. He had to force himself to treat Marilyn as she needed to be treated—as someone who was in real danger of coronary disaster.

But the questions stayed in the back of his mind. There was so much he wanted to know.

Dr Ally Westruther…

He knew so little, but the more he found out, the more he wanted to discover.

CHAPTER FOUR

BY THE time Darcy reached the refuge, it was ten at night. Maybe they'd be settled, he thought. Most of the lights were out. The big central room was still illuminated, however, and he walked in to find Ally standing in front of the fireplace. Someone had lit a fire and the crackle and glow of the flames was a warmth all by itself.

There was a woman in an armchair before the fire. Lorraine? Ally was standing behind her, gently running her fingers through her hair.

The scene was so different to the chaos of the afternoon that he stopped short in astonishment. Lorraine looked almost asleep, her head tilted back and her eyes closed.

Ally looked across at him and smiled, but her fingers kept on with their dreamy rub.

'Here's Dr Rochester,' she said softly. 'Come to check on all of us. Too late. Everyone's asleep, Dr Rochester, except for Lorraine and she soon will be.'

I would be, too, Darcy thought, dazed, if those hands did that to me.

'The kids?' he managed, and Ally's smile deepened. There was huge personal satisfaction for her in this day's work, he thought, though he couldn't understand why.

'They're washed and fed and settled. Tommy and Deidre and Lilly and baby Dot. I've checked them all. There's no signs of illness, though all of them are still bearing their chickenpox scars.'

'I need to check.'

'I don't want you waking them.'

'You want me to accept your word?'

'I do.' She was still calmly massaging Lorraine's head, running her hands through the woman's newly washed hair again and again. Lorraine's hair was a nondescript brown, normally plaited, greasy and dull. Now it hung down her back in soft, shimmering waves. The woman's face, strained and distressed every time Darcy had seen her, now looked years younger.

'Isn't she pretty?' Ally asked, as if guessing his thoughts. And then, as Lorraine cautiously opened her eyes, Ally let her hands drop to Lorraine's shoulders. 'Better?'

'You can't believe how much,' Lorraine whispered. 'You're sure... We... He can't...'

'I'd imagine Jerry's in jail and likely to stay that way,' Ally told her.

'But without him...'

'Without him you'll do very well. You and Penny and Margaret are firm friends and the kids love each other. There's no need to separate. You can pool your pensions and live happily ever after, somewhere where you don't have to cart water or go without food or put your kids at risk. Isn't that right Dr Rochester?'

'That's right.' Darcy was still struggling with the sensation that he was out of time—out of space. 'Um…the men?'

'Robert and Greg are sleeping in the other wing,' she told him. 'Robert's face is the biggest worry. It'll need attention almost straightaway. I was hoping you might be here soon enough to give him something for the pain, but after a hot shower and a big dinner he thought he might go to sleep anyway. I gave him as much paracetamol as I could.'

'You…'

'I don't think it's affecting the eye yet,' she told him, seemingly oblivious to his astonishment. 'But you need to see him first thing in the morning.'

'You're organising me?'

'Yes, Doctor,' she said meekly—and to his absolute astonishment, Lorraine giggled.

A giggle.

Since Sam's death he'd been going up to the ridge once a month, whether they liked it or not, checking on the children. In all of that time he hadn't seen so much as a smile.

And here was a giggle.

He stared at her as if he couldn't believe it. He *couldn't* believe it. A butterfly emerging from an ugly grey chrysalis.

'Is Marigold OK?' Lorraine asked, but there wasn't the desperate concern he'd assumed she'd have for her daughter. Ally's massage almost seemed to have her drugged. 'And Jody and David?'

'They're fine,' he told her. 'Jody's settling. We've put Marigold on intravenous antibiotics and I think her arm should show signs of recovery within twenty-four hours. She's already asleep. And David was sitting up in bed drinking a thick-shake as I left him.'

'There,' Ally said in quiet satisfaction. 'All fixed. Didn't I tell you Dr Rochester was wonderful? A real-life hero. With a name like Darcy Rochester, what do you expect?'

She smiled at him. They were both smiling at him. The look they were giving him was a sort of female conspiratorial look, like he was...some sort of hunk on the front of a romance novel?

Good grief. He had to get out of here, he thought desperately. Any minute now he'd start to blush.

But Ally was moving on. 'I'll show you where you're sleeping,' she said to Lorraine, breaking a silence which suddenly seemed to Darcy to be almost unbearable. 'Do you think you'll sleep?'

'Of course I'll sleep,' the woman told her. 'And you don't need to show me. I've already seen. You know, there's an electric blanket on my bed? Oh, the warmth.' Lorraine rose on legs that were a little shaky. She'd turned from admiring Darcy—much to Darcy's relief—and now she gripped Ally's hands. 'I don't know how to thank you.'

'I only did what you would have done yourselves in a day or two,' Ally told her, and Darcy thought that, no, she was wrong there, but maybe it was a way of giving the woman's pride back to her. 'Things just came to a head when I was there. Now, you're not to worry. You know the kids are safe. The future will be taken care of. Elsa's coming back in the morning to talk practicalities with all of you, but everything's going to be better. I promise.'

'Oh, my dear.'

'Go to bed, Lorraine,' Ally said softly. 'Go to sleep. For as long as you want.'

They were left alone.

The marine refuge had been built by the harbour, and the long living room was used by the fishermen as a meeting place when the pub was unsuitable—when they needed clear heads to make decisions. It was filled with big, squashy armchairs, the fire was set in a vast stone fireplace, and the windows looked over the bluff to the lighthouse beyond.

From here they could hear the waves crashing on the shore. The sound of the sea, the crackle of the fire and the fact that the overhead lights were low…it lent the place an intimacy that seemed almost overwhelming.

Darcy stared across at Ally, trying to adjust to what was happening. She was much as he'd met her on the doorstep a few hours ago, but now she'd been in the bush, pushed aside a few chooks, bathed a few kids, hugged some adults. Maybe she'd even wept a bit.

She looked bedraggled, he thought. She looked exhausted and battered and worn. But still she looked…lovely?

'Can I drive you home?'

'That'd be great,' she said faintly, then hesitated. 'How's Jody? Were you telling the truth to Lorraine—that she's settling?'

'It appears so.' For some stupid reason he was having trouble with his voice. She was throwing him off balance and he didn't know why. Jody. Concentrate on Jody. 'Her obs are settling a little.

The fluid is starting to take effect. But, hell, Ally, if we hadn't got her out of there she'd have been dead by this time tomorrow.'

'You would have taken her anyway,' she said slowly. 'You were planning on picking her up and carting her down here, whatever the consequences.'

The only way to answer that was with the truth. 'Yes.'

'I guessed you were. But the fuss... You could have been sued for abduction.'

'Maybe.'

'So I saved you from going to prison.' Her irrepressible smile peeped out. 'How nice. Does that rate another sandwich?'

That took him aback. 'You can't possibly be hungry?'

'Are you kidding?' She glanced at her watch. 'It's five hours since I last ate and that was a mere snack.'

He thought about the food she'd put away and he grinned. 'Yeah. An appetiser. Didn't you eat here?'

'I was bathing kids when the adults were fed, and I was hugging adults when the kids were fed. The lady who runs this place—Cornelia, is it?— didn't think of feeding me.'

'I'll take you home now.'

'Fat lot of good that'll do.' She dug into her pocket and produced two banknotes. 'These are a real mockery at ten at night when every store in the place is closed. And I so wanted a steak.' She sounded mournful.

'You don't have anything at home?' he asked, startled.

'I have my grocery money right here,' she said with dignity. 'I was planning on shopping when you picked me up.'

Hey! 'I did not pick you up.'

'What else do you call it? You ruined my plans. You interfered with my shopping.'

'Surely you have an egg or something.'

She glowered. 'I have tea bags.'

He choked. 'Yum.'

'Yeah. So take me home. My tea bags are waiting.' She managed a martyr's groan. 'But who am I to complain? After all, I have my satisfaction to keep me warm.'

'You really enjoyed sending Jerry to jail?'

Her smile this time was genuine. 'You don't know how much. It's worth every tummy rumble.'

'Are you going to tell me about Jerry?'

'You know about Jerry.'

'Only what he's done here. That won't get him put in jail.'

'No.' She smiled again, and her smile was suddenly tinged with sadness. 'And it's so hard to get a conviction. But they won't let him go. Not with what I've told them. He won't even get out on bail with his previous record for absconding.'

'So how do you know him?' he asked curiously. They were standing before the open fire in a strange setting of forced intimacy and he thought she might tell him things now that she otherwise wouldn't. And suddenly he badly wanted to know.

'My parents were mixed up with him,' she told him.

'Yeah?'

'Yeah,' she said flatly. The fire spat behind her and a log rolled forward onto the grate. She walked forward to push it back with the poker and he frowned.

'You're limping.'

'I'm not limping.'

'You're limping.'

'You're imagining it.'

He stared down at her feet—to the inappropriate flip-flops. And he remembered something that had been pushed into the background amongst the drama up on the ridge.

Jerry kicking a pile of firewood. A branch swinging forward with a resounding thump against Ally's foot.

'He hurt you.'

'Jerry can't hurt me.'

'Sit down, Ally,' he told her.

'I'm not—'

He put his hands on her shoulders and propelled her backward into the chair Lorraine had just vacated. He flicked on the reading light beside the chair and a pool of light illuminated her slight frame.

She looked really young, he thought suddenly. And really…scared?

'Hey, I won't hurt you.'

'I know you won't hurt me,' she said with some indignation. 'Let me up.' She tried to rise but his hands gripped her again and held.

'Stay.'

'Like a dog.' She glowered.

'If you like. Behave. Let me see your foot.'

'There's nothing wrong.'

But he was kneeling before her, flicking the flip-flop from her foot and raising it to the light.

'Ouch.'

'That's my line,' she told him.

'Well, why aren't you using it?' He shifted her foot a little so the light was better, grimacing. 'Hell, Ally, there's a massive splinter in here.'

'Gee, that makes me feel better,' she retorted. 'I know I have a splinter. I'll dig it out when I have a shower.'

'It's too deep.'

'It wouldn't be deep if you hadn't said massive,' she said, and her voice was suddenly a trifle unsure. 'How massive?'

'You haven't looked?'

'When would I have had time to look?' She grabbed her foot from him and bent it up so she was peering at her heel. It was such an unguarded gesture. What other woman he knew would do that? He stared at her vulnerable head, bent over her foot, and he felt something inside tug. Hard.

'Ouch is right.' She stared for a moment longer and then put her foot down. 'But it'll come out.'

'I'll see to it now.'

'I'll see to it myself.'

'Ally, I don't think it's going to come out with a pair of tweezers,' he told her. 'It's deep and long and it looks as if it's in parts. I'll give you a local anaesthetic and get the thing fully cleaned.'

'You'll do no such thing.'

'Oh, right.' He stood back and fixed her with a goaded look. 'So you've gone to all that trouble to save Jody from infection, yet you sail into infection yourself—all because you're scared of a local anaesthetic.'

'I'm not scared.'

'Good girl,' he told her, and grabbed his bag.

'Hey!'

'Shut up. I'm working,' he told her.

'I can—'

'You can't.' He lifted her foot again, inspected it carefully, then sighed and rose to fetch a bowl of warm water from the sink at the side of the room.

She half rose as if to leave.

He turned and gazed at her—holding her eyes with his.

She glowered again—and then sank back into her chair.

'You think you're so indispensable,' she muttered.

'Maybe I am.' He smiled. 'I can't imagine you massaging a splinter out of a foot.'

'No, but—'

'And there's not a single essential oil that has splinter removal as one of its properties.'

'Oh, shut up,' she told him.

He grinned. 'You could at least be grateful.'

'I'm grateful.'

'Good.' He came back to her and started loading a syringe. 'This might sting a little.'

'Yeah, yeah. I know exactly what "sting a little" means when it's a needle into your foot. It means sending me through the roof.'

'You need a bullet to bite,' he told her, and she grimaced.

'I'd rather have steak. This is not turning out to be my day, Dr Rochester.'

'But you have put Jerry in jail.'

'There is that,' she said, brightening a little.

'OK.' He swabbed the side of her foot, waited until he could see she was ready and then injected.

She bit her lip—hard—and then nodded.

'Fine.'

'Good girl.'

'Don't patronise me.'

'I would never patronise you, Ally,' he told her. 'I think you're wonderful.'

Her eyes flew wide at that. 'Really?'

'Really.'

'Wonders will never cease.'

He grinned. 'OK. Give the injection a few minutes to take effect. In the meantime…tell me about you and Jerry.'

For a while he thought she wouldn't tell him. She sat with her foot stretched out on a stool before the fire and she looked…blank. It hurt, he thought, and it wasn't her foot that was doing it.

Would she tell?

He continued to wait, but the combination of firelight and the sound of the sea was almost hypnotic, and finally she started. Her face was still blank. It was as if she was recounting something that had happened to others. Not to her.

'My father was associated with Jerry long before I was born,' she told him. 'Jerome…Jerry…well, you've seen him. His personality is overwhelming. Dad met him here when they were both boys. Jerry used to come down here when his father was checking his properties. When Dad went to the city to live, he caught up with Jerry again, and finally he went to live with him. Jerry's father had given him a farm in the hills above Nimbin in New South Wales. That was the start. You've seen the men who were with Jerry. My dad was like that.'

He knew. Damn, he knew.

'And your mother?' He'd started washing her foot with the warm water, carefully removing the soil of the day. She appeared hardly to notice. She was intent on her story.

'Dad met my mother here,' she told him. 'Dad was twenty years older than she was, and he'd left town before she was born. But Dad had to come back here to fix up something to do with his parents' estate and he met my mother then. She was only fifteen and he got her pregnant. My grandfather was furious. He wasn't…he wasn't a forgiving man, my grandfather. He demanded she have an abortion and she ran away with my father. So for the first few years of my life I was with Jerry and his people.'

She'd lived as these people had. She knew.

He hesitated. 'Jerry… Was Jerry all right with you?'

She frowned. 'You mean, did he abuse me? No. To be honest, I don't remember much about my early childhood. All I know is that when I was four my mother brought me back here. She didn't explain why. She seemed afraid but Grandpa didn't know why and she insisted on going back herself. Whether she was still in love with Dad, or whether she was under Jerry's spell, I don't know. But she had enough sense to be afraid for me. Anyway, she left me with my grandfather and I stayed with him for eight years.'

'And then?'

She sighed. 'Then my grandfather died and my father took me back.'

'Your mother…'

'By that time she was just a victim,' she said wearily. 'She did what everyone told her. She'd stood up to them once when she'd taken me to my grandfather, but she was incapable of standing up to them again.'

Darcy was totally focussed on her story—but he had to concentrate on the procedure he was undertaking. He lifted her foot and lightly ran his nail down either side of her sole. 'Can you feel this?'

'No.'

'Nothing?'

'No.'

'Good. I'm starting.' He inspected the wound with care and then reached for a scalpel. She looked down at what he was doing and then carefully closed her eyes.

Good choice. And he could distract her still further with her story.

'So you stayed with Jerry from the time you were twelve?' he asked as he carefully split the skin at the side of the wood. The more hc saw the more he was astonished. She'd walked on the splinter for hours. It must have been agony. It had shattered into pieces and was deeply embedded.

How had she done it?

But she was focussed on her childhood. Had she stayed with Jerry?

'Are you kidding?' She smiled, albeit a shaky one. 'I had no choice. I was twelve and I went where I was taken. But Jerry was in trouble. Once, when he was really desperate, he came here and he brought me with him. He knew this place was deserted and there was some sort of drug deal going on. I was supposed to sit on the ridge and watch for people coming. For about three days he hid up there, and I was desperately lonely. All that time I knew my home was here—the people I knew—and, oh, I wanted to come back.'

'You could have come.'

'How? My grandfather wasn't here any more. I didn't know who would help me. I figured my father would just come and get me again. No. I was stuck. But while I was up on the ridge I was furious, with all the righteous indignation of a lonely twelve-year-old who was dragged where she didn't want to be. I used to watch Jerry. I knew he was doing something illegal. I watched where he hid stuff. I memorised everyone who came. I took car registrations. I eavesdropped and I figured things out. From that time on, I kept careful records of everything I could. But of course Mum and Dad were part of the community. I didn't see how I could do anything without destroying them.' She swallowed and darted him a look that was suddenly unsure.

Darcy stayed intent on her foot. He was carefully manoeuvring pieces of shattered wood out and he needed to concentrate, but he also knew he had to give her space.

'Then...' she whispered. 'Then Jerry decided I was old enough...'

Enough. Her voice trailed off to nothing.

Darcy's hands stilled. His heart seemed to still. 'Ally...'

But he might have known this was no passive victim. Not Ally.

'Only I wasn't,' she told him, her voice suddenly defiant. 'Grandpa had taught me karate—how cool is that?—and I fought. I took off into the scrub round the horrible place we were staying, and I ran. It took me hours to get to the nearest town but when I arrived I talked and talked and I don't know why they believed me but they did. I was scratched and bruised and starving and just...vitriolic. In the end the police went up and arrested Jerry.'

He was dumbfounded. 'You had him arrested?' He shook his head in disbelief, seeing her as she must have been then. A twelve-year-old, up against the world. There was a lump in the back of his throat and he had to fight to speak again. 'Guns blazing?' he ventured, trying desperately for lightness. He wanted to hit someone. He desperately wanted to hit someone. Maybe it was just as well he hadn't known this when he'd faced Jerry.

'Hardly.' She gave a rueful chuckle. 'Not quite. Though if there'd been guns handy, who knows?' She shrugged and in an unconscious echo of his own thoughts she added, 'Maybe it was just as well I only knew karate. Anyway, it didn't help. He skipped bail and left the country. Leaving a mess.' She stared down into his angry eyes and ventured a lopsided smile. 'Um… Dr Rochester, do you think you could concentrate on my foot?'

He caught himself. He was operating here. He went back to the splinter but it was almost clear. All he had to do was clean it really thoroughly.

He started to wash it out. As he concentrated on medicine again his voice came under control and it seemed possible to ask more questions.

'What happened to your parents?'

'They weren't my parents any more,' she said sadly, staring down at her foot. 'They weren't capable of caring for themselves, let alone me. I went into foster care. End of story.'

Only it wasn't. He glanced up into her face, and behind the satisfaction that this day had given her he saw more.

She was haunted, he thought. He'd treated her as a flibbertigibbet, a person who'd bowled into town with her sky-blue signs and her ideas of making a living from massage.

And she had such shadows.

'No one knew,' he said, forcing himself to stay focussed on the dressing he was applying. 'No one in the town seemed to have any idea of what happened to you.'

'My grandfather never talked,' she told him. 'He was a hard man. He never talked of anything. Jerome Hatfield was our personal tragedy.'

'Yet…'

'Enough,' she said, almost roughly. 'My foot's fine.' He'd taped the dressing in place and her foot was as good as it was going to get. 'Take me home, Dr Rochester. Even a tea bag's looking good.'

'How up to date are you with your tetanus shots?'

'I'm fine. I had a booster two years back.'

'Try to keep the weight off your heel.'

'I've been doing that all evening. I'm an expert.'

'Right.' He hesitated. He should drive her home. But he couldn't let her go home to a tea bag. Could he?

No.

'Let me find you a steak,' he said, and there was a short silence.

'You could do that?'

'I have half a dozen steaks in my freezer. My microwave can defrost them in minutes.'

'I thought you had a wood stove.'

'Yep. A wood stove and a microwave. How about that?'

'You want me to go to your place?'

'My dogs make great chaperones. And…' he ventured a smile '…I hear you know karate.'

'And two other Japanese words. That makes me bilingual. Or trilingual. Something.'

He grinned again. She was stunning, he thought. He was appropriately stunned. 'OK. If all your patients are asleep, let's go.'

'They're not my patients.'

'I'm not so sure,' he said faintly. 'I'm starting to feel superfluous.'

'Not when you have six steaks in your freezer. You're not superfluous at all.'

'There you go, then.' His smile faded. 'Not completely superfluous. But definitely completely confused.' He hesitated. 'You gave Robert paracetamol?'

'Let's check him,' she told him, meeting his concern before he'd voiced it. 'I can wait that long. Of all of them, Robert's the one who'll be awake. That carcinoma is almost bone-deep.'

He cast her an odd look. 'You know your medical stuff.'

'We get it in massage school.'

'How to treat carcinoma?'

'How to recognise one.'

'Massage school's changed since my day.'

'You're how old?' She shrugged. 'OK, Dr Greybeard. Let's check Robert. My tummy's rumbling.'

Robert was asleep, but not deeply. Ally pushed open his bedroom door and he stirred a little, whimpering with pain.

'He hasn't even had an aspirin before tonight,' she whispered in sudden anger, moving across to stare down at him in the soft light cast by the hall lamp. 'His face... It would have been a tiny thing to get rid of a couple of years back, but now...the mess...'

Darcy crossed to stand beside her. She was right. He'd only seen Robert's face in the distance before this. Social Services had forced Jerry to accept him examining the children but the adults had the right to refuse treatment and none of them had come near him.

And now what must have started off as a tiny basal cell carcinoma had spread, covering Robert's forehead and half his cheek. Horrid.

But as far as he could see it hadn't invaded his eye. And it looked clean.

'I washed it and put a mild antiseptic on it,' Ally told him. 'I hope it isn't too deep—that the eye is OK. Even now, he must be facing major surgery. He's so afraid. I talked to him about skin grafts, though. I told him I'm sure there are things that can be done to help.'

Here it was again. Her knowledge of medicine.

Was she a med-school dropout? he wondered. Or somehow trained and deregistered? If so, her use of the word 'doctor' was not only illegal but dangerous.

But this wasn't the time to question it. Robert moaned softly again and Darcy came to a decision.

'I'll wake him. He's only sleeping now because he's exhausted. That pain will wake him up as soon as the exhaustion eases.'

'Morphine and a sedative?'

He raised his brows and she raised hers back.

'Right,' he said, deciding not to take it further.

'I thought Lorraine and Penny might need sedatives to help them sleep,' she told him. 'But a massage worked better. I can't see Robert accepting a massage, though.'

'No,' he said dryly, and he put his hand on the man's shoulder.

'Robert.'

The man woke as if someone was striking him. There was pure terror in his eyes, and he hauled back, cringing. He was a little man, in his mid-forties maybe, but so emaciated he might be much older. His ginger hair was thinning. It had been roughly cut, as if done by himself without the help of a mirror. He wouldn't be out of place in a shelter for homeless men, Darcy thought as he moved swiftly to reassure him.

'It's OK, Robert,' he told him. 'I'm the doctor.'

The man's eyes moved past him and found Ally—and he visibly relaxed. How had this woman achieved their trust in such a short time?

'I'm sorry. I'm sorry, I thought it was…'

'You thought it was Jerry,' Ally finished for him. 'He's in jail, Robert. You know that.'

'I should have gone with him.'

'No,' Ally said fiercely. She sat on the bed and took the little man's hands between hers, her hold compelling. 'There's no ''should'' about it. Jerry tells everyone what to do, and because he's so big and loud and compelling everyone just does it without asking questions. But you've been in agony for months. Jerry hasn't let Dr Rochester help you. Now he can. He's here and he can stop the pain and let you have a decent night's sleep.'

'The bed's pretty good,' the man whispered, and Ally gave him a smile brimming with encouragement.

'Yep. And so was dinner. And so's the treatment Dr Rochester can give your face. I cleaned it but I've probably made it hurt even more.'

'It's OK,' the man faltered, but Darcy looked at the lines of strain around his eyes and knew he was lying.

'Will you let me give you something for the pain?'

'Ally gave me tablets.'

'Did they help?'

'A little.'

'I can give you something stronger. And if you'll let me,' Darcy said softly, not wanting to bring the terror back into the man's eyes, 'in the next couple of days I'll arrange for you to be transported to one of the big Melbourne hospitals. That face needs a top surgeon to treat it.'

'It's too late. It's spread too far.'

'No.' Darcy made his voice flat and absolutely definite. Ally moved to let Darcy take her place, and he stooped to have a really good look. 'Robert, I don't know how deep it is, but it certainly looks like basal cell carcinoma. That's skin cancer normally caused by sun damage. It's close to the eye but it's not so close that it's going to interfere with either the eye or the eyelid. If we move now, we can fix it. What the surgeon will need to do is cut away the damaged surface. Because it's big, he'll need to do a skin graft. That'll involve taking a piece of skin, probably from somewhere like your thigh, and stitching it over your face so the wound will heal.'

'Ally told me that. But it'll never heal.'

'It will,' Ally said. 'Believe us. You must believe us, Robert. We can make this better.'

'But I can't afford—'

'The public health system will cover this,' Darcy told him. 'Because it's so close to your eye you'll be treated as a priority patient. If I send you to Melbourne in the next couple of days, you'll be operated on almost immediately.'

'And...and after that?'

'You can be brought back here to recuperate if you wish,' Darcy told him. 'We'll put your residence down as care of this place, and take it from there. Our social worker will talk to you tomorrow about appropriate housing, and whether you want to stay with the others or not.' Then, as Robert's eyes grew confused, he put his hands on his shoulders and pressed him back on the pillows.

'Enough,' he told him. 'Too much has happened too fast. But will you allow me to give you an injection? Something that will have you pain-free and let you sleep for the rest of the night?'

'Pain-free? All night?'

'Magic,' Darcy said with a wry grin. He gave a sideways wink at Ally. 'You know, even though massage therapists can solve most of the problems

of the world, there's still a use for us doctors. Can
I give you the injection, mate?'

Robert looked from Ally to Darcy and back
again. His face said he was confused beyond belief. But the terror had faded.

He'd been given hope. It had been worth waking
him up, Darcy thought. He'd have woken in the
small hours to pain and to the knowledge that the
cancer was spreading. He must have been doing
so for months. Waiting for the cancer to reach his
eyes, and then…

That was the way of madness.

But instead of madness, now there was hope. He
gazed at the two of them and then his weary face
broke into the ghost of what might once have been
a smile.

'Maybe you're crazy, the pair of you,' he muttered. 'And why don't I care? Go ahead, Doc. Give
me the injection. Work your magic.'

CHAPTER FIVE

ALLY felt like she was floating. Not in a good way, though, she decided as Darcy ushered her once more into his luxurious car. Too much had happened to her this day for her to take it all on board.

Her hatred of Jerome Hatfield had built over the years to a point where she hadn't been able to handle it. She'd taken drastic steps in her life and moved on. She'd thought. Then today the memories had slammed back with such force that she felt as if everything had been sucked out of her. Her feet were no longer grounded. She felt…ill.

'How's your foot?'

'It's fine,' she whispered. 'Just fine.'

'You can't take this all in,' Darcy said gently, and she stared across at him as if she didn't recognise him.

'It doesn't change anything,' she murmured. 'To be given the opportunity to stop Jerry doing more damage… That's fine but he's done so much damage already.'

'To your family?'

'To everyone.' She hesitated. 'Thank you, though, for taking me up there this afternoon. Of all the lucky breaks.'

'If the police have been looking for him for so long, I can't believe they didn't look here.'

'He went overseas years and years ago,' she said. 'The trail was cold. The police couldn't check every one of his father's properties all the time on the off chance that he'd come back.'

'But when Social Services checked...'

'If he was using another name, there'd be no connection. If you didn't contact the police...'

'There was no reason to,' he said grimly. 'He wasn't breaking the law. The children, though... If there's been abuse that we missed...'

'I doubt it,' she said. 'Jerry didn't want me— that way—until I reached puberty, and all these kids are younger.' She stared ahead into the dark. 'I suspect he's infertile. None of the kids is ever his. He picks up dysfunctional families like mine, or single mums who have babies. Then he acts as if he's the kids' father. Until they reach their teens.'

'I should have—'

'You shouldn't have done anything,' she said gently. 'You contacted Social Services when Sam died. You checked the kids every month. And you took me up there this afternoon. So stop beating yourself up. I'm doing enough of that for both of us.'

'You...'

'You know, when I was twelve, I was standing above him up on a cliff when he was having a bush shower. There was a huge rock lying just at my feet and I thought, What if it moved?' She managed a smile. 'But I didn't move the rock and he went on to destroy more lives.' She shrugged. 'Anyway, let's not talk about him. Let's concentrate on my steak.'

'The important things in life.'

'Right.'

Darcy lived in a weatherboard cottage set to the side of the Tambrine Creek hospital. He locked the car and turned to find Ally already opening the gate leading to the back door. The catch was tricky. How...?

'I lived here for years,' she told him, seeing his confusion. 'This is the doctor's house, right? I'm the doctor's grandkid.'

The thought was disorientating. She'd lived here before?

'And I hope you've been looking after it.'

'I have.'

'Let's see.' Then the back door burst open, swung wide from within by the force of two dogs.

Jekyll and Hyde. Jekyll was an ancient black and white but mostly grey cocker spaniel and Hyde was his younger compatriot, a sprightly eight-year-old golden version of the same breed. They bounded down the path with joy.

'Hey, guys.' Darcy squatted to hug them. They submitted and then wheeled to investigate Ally.

She promptly sat on the path and hugged back. Enveloped in a mass of wriggling canine joy, she smiled up at him with delight.

'This is your family. Where are the chooks?'

'Roosting,' he told her. 'And, no, I'm not waking them up for hugs.'

She giggled and hugged the dogs again, struggling to her feet. They were gorgeous. Dogs and girl...

Particularly girl.

For Ally, the sensation that she was coming home was almost overwhelming. Apart from the dogs. Her grandpa had always refused to have a dog. 'Pets interfere with your life,' he'd snapped, and that had been that.

But Darcy had dogs. Gorgeous dogs. She glanced up at him and he was smiling and she thought...

Well, she thought she ought to concentrate on dogs.

Maybe now she could get a dog. Maybe.

There wasn't room in her little apartment above her shop.

Maybe a very small dog?

He was holding the back door wide and she hesitated. She hadn't been here for seventeen years. Despite her grandfather's coldness, she'd loved this place. If it had changed...

It hadn't. She walked into the kitchen and it had hardly changed at all.

Oh, everything was fresh. The room was freshly painted. Shabby gingham curtains had been replaced by new ones. There was a gleaming modern refrigerator and a microwave. But the vast wooden table was the one she'd sat at all those years ago, and her grandmother's old rocker was still in the corner. Her grandpa hadn't liked anyone using it but Ally had snuggled into it when he hadn't been around. In it her mother had seemed closer. She was sure her mother had used the rocker.

And the stove. 'You kept the stove. You make toast on my stove.' She darted across and hauled open the fire-door. Darcy had stoked the stove before he'd left that morning and now it contained a bed of glowing embers. 'I so wanted the stove to be the same. Yum.' She opened the oven door and peered into its black depths. 'I used to put my feet in here every morning all through winter. I had leather slippers and I'd rest my feet in here while I toasted my toast.'

'I still do,' Darcy told her. 'All my toast tastes of ancient footwear.'

And suddenly they were grinning at each other like fools. The tensions and heartache of the day dissipated in this one crazy moment—when he was looking at her with a delight that matched hers. With a grin that...

Whoa.

She forced herself to break eye contact, and she was aware that he did the same, breaking away at the same moment. They could be mature adults and ignore this, she thought frantically.

Ignore what?

Darcy had turned to the fridge and was delving into the freezer.

'Do you need help?' she managed, thrown suddenly right off balance.

'I cook steak and salad just fine. It's my staple diet.'

'You want me to feed the dogs, then?' she asked, and her voice was still stupidly breathless. Damn, how had he done that to her?

'If you would,' he said brusquely. Maybe he was as disconcerted as she was. 'Their food's in the container on the back porch and their bowls are there, too. A cup and a half each and don't let them con you into more.'

'I'm a rigid disciplinarian,' she told him, but she still hadn't got her voice under control. And when she made her way out to the back porch, she couldn't stop the sensation that she felt like she was escaping.

From what? She didn't know. All she knew was that she intended staying out there for a while, ostensibly watching as the dogs enjoyed their dinner but in reality staring out at the night sky, listening to the sea in the background, smelling the night scent of the gums and trying to adjust to the crazy feeling of unreality that was all about her.

Maybe it had been a mistake to come back here. The way she was feeling. The way she was feeling about Darcy?

This was nonsense, she told herself crossly. Just because the man had the most romantic name and he looked like a Hollywood hero...

No. It wasn't that. It was the way he smiled at her. The way he made her feel.

She sat on the back step and hugged her knees. Men didn't make her feel like this. Relationships weren't her scene. The way to survive was to keep herself independent. Heart-whole and fancy-free.

Jekyll finished his dinner and came and nuzzled her hand. She fondled his silky ears and he gazed up with adoration.

'Maybe a very small dog,' she whispered. 'But that's all, Ally Westruther. Anything more would be a disaster and you know it. You have a plan. You stick to it.'

The steak was wonderful. When Darcy called her for dinner she found steaks that almost covered the dinner plate and the first mouthful had her in heaven.

'Yum.'

'You really do enjoy your food.' He gazed at her in fascination.

'Hush,' she said reverentially. 'I'm eating.'

He did hush, but she was aware that he was watching her as she ate, and there were still questions in his eyes.

Hadn't she told him enough? For heaven's sake…

If he asked her more she just might tell him, she thought ruefully. Sitting here in this room, with the hiss of the old kettle on the wood stove in the background as it had been in the background all her childhood. It undermined her defences and left her feeling as if there was nowhere to go.

In desperation she gazed around the room, searching for the personal. Something that would tell her something about this man and take the attention from her. Deflect it to him.

There was a photograph on the mantelpiece. It was of a young woman with deep chestnut curls, a wide smiling face, laughing grey eyes. Lovely.

'Who's that?' she asked, and he turned to look as if he wasn't sure who might have been photographed and sitting on his mantelpiece. Then he turned back to his steak.

'That's my wife.'

She thought about it. She ate a bit more steak.

'That's your wife,' she repeated at last. 'You mean…as in present tense?'

'She's dead. She died six years ago.'

Ally flinched. 'I'm sorry.'

'Yeah.'

Some people would stop there, Ally thought ruefully, but when had she ever stopped when going on could get her into trouble? It was her life skill.

'How did she die?'

'Leukaemia.'

'Bummer.'

'As you say.'

'Was that why you came here?' she asked. 'To get away from an old life?'

'Maybe.'

'Was she a doctor, too?'

'She was, as a matter of fact,' he said, and he glanced back at the photograph again as if reminding himself of who she was. 'We were married in med school.'

'And when she died you bolted here.'

'I wouldn't have put it like that.'

'No,' she said thoughtfully. 'But it's a good place to bolt to.'

'If you like hard work.'

'And you do?'

'I like the medicine I'm doing,' he told her. 'But…'

'But?'

'I hate it when I'm in trouble,' he admitted. 'I had a woman with a disastrous birth last month. I can't do obstetrics—with no back-up I send all my mums to the city a couple of weeks before the birth. But Cindy had no intention of going and I couldn't make her. She went into labour and didn't call me. By the time she did, she'd been in labour for almost thirty hours and the baby was in dire trouble. I did a forceps delivery but the baby was born flat. An Apgar score of two. Hell, I needed a paediatrician and an anaesthetist and a specialist nursery—and I had nothing. I got the flying squad in—a team of specialists who retrieve babies in trouble in country areas—but it was far too late. She lost the baby.'

There was such anger in his voice. Fury.

'If you hadn't been here...' she said softly.

'Yeah, I know. If I hadn't been here then Cindy would have died as well as the baby. But it made me feel foul.'

'Hey.' She reached across the table and put her hand over his. It was an involuntary gesture and why she'd made it she didn't know. All she knew was that she'd had to. 'You can't save the world.'

'No.' He looked up and managed a smile. 'I know I can't. But I can try.'

'Maybe you could try a massage some time,' she said, half-smiling, and then as she thought about what she'd said, she thought, Was she nuts? 'Not with me, of course,' she said hurriedly. 'But next time you go to the city. It's great for stress.'

She knew he wouldn't. What a stupid thing to say. It sounded like she was drumming up business.

'That was stupid,' she whispered. 'A dopey thing to say. I'm sorry.' Finally she withdrew her hand and watched as he stared down at where her fingers had been. It was like he was confused.

But before he could respond, the phone on his belt interrupted. Darcy gave her an apologetic nod, then left the table to answer it.

Her foot was starting to throb.

She was bone weary, she thought suddenly. Reaction from the events of the day was setting in with a vengeance.

The dogs were snoozing by the stove and she almost envied them. She did envy them. Move over, guys, she thought as Darcy spoke urgently into his phone behind her. I'm with you.

Darcy's voice stopped abruptly. She turned and he was reaching for his bag.

She'd lived for years with her grandpa. She knew trouble when she saw it. His car keys were lying on the sink, and she flipped them to him before he started looking for them.

'Thanks.' He was already moving. 'Sorry. I—'

'You need to go,' she told him. 'Just go.'

'The guy who was arrested with Jerry,' he snapped as he hauled open the back door. 'He's tried to suicide in his police cell. They're cutting him down now.'

There was nothing to do.

She tried to let her mind go blank. It didn't work.

More destruction. She'd had Jerry arrested and someone had decided to suicide because of it.

No. He'd have been suicidal anyway, she told herself, turning on taps so violently the water splashcd up and onto thc floor.

The memories were overwhelming. Her father...

By the time Jerry had been arrested when she'd been twelve, her father had had no self-esteem at all. He'd drifted away, a ghost with no hope of regaining any shred of life. He'd died soon after and she'd hated the thought that she'd caused it.

'This isn't your fault,' she whispered into the washing-up water. 'He brought it on all of them and you've done your best to set them free. If it's too late...'

She was crying, she realised, tears dripping into the suds and she gave her cheeks an angry swipe. Jekyll came over and sniffed her ankles and she gave up on the washing-up and sat down to hug him.

'I'm definitely getting a dog.'

The phone rang.

It'd be the ambulance boys, seeing if Darcy was on his way, Ally thought, or the policeman panicking and saying hurry up. Either way there was nothing to be gained by answering it. Darcy should be there by now.

The ringing stopped. Another ringing took its place.

It was a different tone.

She struggled to her feet and checked the phone. It was the fixed line that was ringing now, the instrument on the wall by the door. The first ring must have been to Darcy's cell phone—which was lying on the kitchen table.

He'd dropped his cell phone as he'd run.

No matter. He was on his way.

But…

He should be there by now, she thought. His car had screamed out of the driveway and it was only five or six blocks to the police station. He'd be there, trying desperately to resuscitate the suicide.

So who was ringing?

She lifted the phone like it was a loaded gun, and a woman's hysterical voice sounded down the line. 'Dr Rochester, thank God. Marilyn Lewis has arrested. Intensive Care. Now!'

The phone went dead.

This wasn't a good moment.

Ally let the receiver drop.

Marilyn Lewis.

She remembered Marilyn. Once upon a time Marilyn had run the general store, and there had always been a lolly for Ally.

Ally's childhood friend, Sue, was Marilyn's daughter. Ally had lost touch with the family, but she remembered them with deep affection. Marilyn making scones after school. Marilyn hugging her when her grandpa had been particularly cold. Marilyn tucking her into bed with Sue when Grandpa had been called out at night.

After all these years, to meet again like this.

There was no choice. After all her agonising there was no choice at all.

Ally dropped the dishcloth and, sore foot or not, she started to run.

What met her was chaos.

There were two nurses on duty, and clearly both of them were panicking. One, a middle-aged woman, was standing by a bed with a stethoscope—a great help that was—and a younger male was trying to hook up a cardiac monitor. His fingers seemed nerveless, and he looked up as she entered with something akin to desperation.

'Dr R...' His voice trailed off. 'You're not...'

Of course she wasn't Dr Rochester. But she was already in the room, edging aside the nurse with the stethoscope and doing a fast visual assessment. Marilyn looked ashen, and there was no movement. Her eyes were wide and she was staring straight upward, seeing nothing.

'How long?' she snapped, and the male nurse fought to answer.

'Four…five minutes. Leonie was watching her but she went to the bathroom. I was on supper break. I just stepped out.'

'History of heart condition?'

'Yes. Two…two minor heart attacks and angina. Heart pain tonight.'

Why the hell wasn't the monitor attached, then? 'Get that monitor working—fast.' She glanced around the room. It was tiny—Tambrine Creek's answer to Intensive Care was a far cry from a big city hospital's set-up—but there was everything she needed.

But first…

'Marilyn,' she said strongly, taking the older woman's shoulders and giving her an urgent shake. 'Marilyn, can you hear me?' It was a remote hope that this was a temporary loss of consciousness that she could snap out of, but patients had woken before, and Marilyn wouldn't thank her for broken ribs if this wasn't a cardiac arrest.

There was no response.

Airway.

She rolled Marilyn onto her side, not waiting for one of the nurses to help her. The older nurse was actually wringing her hands. Of all the useless actions. But she didn't have time to complain.

What she was doing now was almost intuitive, drilled into her over and over again. ABC. Airways. Breathing. Circulation.

Her mouth was clear. Her tongue wasn't blocking her throat. Airway fine.

Breathing.

She put her hand on Marilyn's breast. Her chest wasn't moving.

'Mask,' she snapped, and held out a hand. Her other hand was searching for a pulse. Nothing. 'Get that monitor hooked up fast.'

The younger nurse—his label said his name was Paul—was fighting to connect it. He at least seemed vaguely competent.

'Mask,' she snapped again, and the older nurse finally managed to turn to the trolley and fetch it. Ally still had to snatch the mask from her hands. She fitted it with lightning precision, inserting the Guedel airway with a speed learned from scores of practise sessions on dummies and a few more on the real thing.

She fitted the bag and squeezed, then stared down at Marilyn's chest. Damn, she couldn't see. Marilyn was wearing some sort of frilly nightgown.

She put her hand in the neckline and ripped the frills to the waist.

She pushed the bag again.

Marilyn's chest heaved—and fell.

The airway was clear. That meant this really was heart and not obstruction caused by swallowing.

Ally started rolling her, but Paul was with her now, helping. 'Monitor's up,' he told her, and Ally's eyes flicked to the cabinet where the tiny screen was located.

The line wasn't absolutely straight. It was a faint vibration, hardly going above the horizontal, but it was definitely moving.

Ventricular fibrillation.

'We have a chance,' she breathed. 'Paul...'

He knew what to do. He was a competent nurse, Ally decided, just somehow thrown off course by what had been happening. His hands were already linked as she said his name, and before it was completely uttered he was starting the rhythmic thump of cardiac pulmonary resuscitation. She heard a crack and winced. A rib. No matter. It couldn't be allowed to matter.

'Breathe for me,' she snapped to the other nurse.

'But...you're the masseuse,' the woman floundered.

'I'm a doctor. Take the bag, damn you.' Then, as the nurse still didn't respond, she reached over and slapped her. Not hard, but hard enough to wake her up out of the trance. 'Move!'

The woman jolted into action. She didn't have a choice. She took the bag and started the pushing that would keep oxygen entering Marilyn's body.

Ally was fitting electrodes, working around Paul's hands. Everything she needed was there, thank God. She grabbed the paddles and smeared them with jelly.

Right.

She lifted the paddles and placed them just off Marilyn's chest.

'Back,' she ordered.

Paul lifted his hands clear and Ally let the paddles contact Marilyn's bare skin.

Her body gave a convulsive heave.

All eyes went to the monitor.

Nothing.

Paul thumped again and the other nurse—Leonie?—went back to bagging air in. They were in rhythm now, doing what they were trained to do.

'Back.'

The paddles moved into position again.

Another heave.

Nothing.

Again.

Again.

Still the heart monitor told them there was hope. It wasn't the flat line of a completely dead heart. It was still ventricular fibrillation.

'Again!'

Another heave.

The line moved.

Ally was scarcely breathing herself. This so seldom worked. But... The blue line on the monitor was jerking upward. Over and over. Rhythmically.

'We have a beat,' she whispered.

It was time to take a deep breath herself. How long since she'd breathed?

They weren't out of the woods yet.

'Get that oxygen up to maximum,' she snapped as Paul started to speak. How long had the brain been starved?

Marilyn. She stared down at the elderly lady and here came the prayer that seemed to be with her all her working life. Please.

Please.

And, as if in answer, a visible shudder through the old lady's body. Another. And then...

A rasping breath.

Dear God.

Marilyn was breathing in earnest now, her chest moving all by itself. It was the best sight. Her breathing sounded dreadful, a ragged rasping as if it was being torn from her body, but to Ally it was a fantastic sound.

And then the elderly lady's eyes flickered open. They were pain-filled and confused. She attempted to shake her head, trying to rid herself of a mask she didn't understand, gagging a little on the airway, but Ally took her hand and held it, lifting the airway clear but replacing the mask so the oxygen still flowed.

'Marilyn, lie still. It's Ally. You've had a heart attack. You're OK, but you need to lie still.'

Marilyn's eyes focussed. And then, unbelievably, she tried to smile. Her mouth moved beneath the mask.

'Ally.'

'It's me.' Then, as Marilyn's face contorted in pain, Ally looked up at the nurses.

'Get me five milligrams of morphine.'

Silence.

She looked up again and the nurses were glancing at each other in confusion.

'Get me five milligrams of morphine,' she said again, this time through gritted teeth. 'And let's not talk about acting improperly here. Let's not talk about anything at all. I want a syringe of morphine and I want it now. Any questions?'

Paul looked at her for a long moment—and then his mouth twisted in a wry grimace.

'Anything you say—*Doctor*,' he said softly, and went to fetch it.

Ally stayed by Marilyn's side for the next twenty minutes. Reaction was setting in, but she wasn't undoing her good work by leaving. She set up an intravenous drip and watched like a hawk. But at the end of twenty minutes the morphine was working. The monitor was showing a steady, reassuring beat of a heart that was working well. Somehow they seemed to have done it.

Leonie had disappeared to somewhere else in the hospital but Paul stayed close. A couple of times he opened his mouth to ask questions but she simply shook her head. She wasn't up to answering questions.

And she knew she didn't have the answers.

Finally she heard what she'd been waiting for. A car drew up outside the hospital and then another, and she heard the sound of Leonie's greeting and Darcy's barked response.

She wasn't ready to face Darcy. Not now.

She'd done what she had to do. She wasn't a doctor any more.

'Take over,' she told Paul, and he nodded. He'd assume she'd be going out to greet Darcy, she thought, but she had no such intention. There was a real doctor here now. She could leave this scene.

And she could. This was her grandpa's hospital. She knew it like the back of her hand.

She walked out the ward door.

Darcy was at the entrance. If she turned to the right she'd run into him.

She turned to the left. She slipped out through the kitchens and into the night. The night was balmy and filled with stars, and the sea was murmuring in the background. But she didn't notice.

Her foot was on fire but she didn't care. The moment she got outside she started to run, and she didn't stop running until she reached her little flat above her rooms. When she got there she slammed the door. Then she leaned against it and started to shake.

She didn't stop shaking for a very long time.

Back at the police station, Sergeant Matheson had done a fine job.

He was a great cop, Darcy thought ruefully as he worked through what had to be done. He'd put Jerry and Kevin, his weedy acolyte, in separate cells and he'd watched them both. A clatter in Kevin's cell had alerted him and he'd gone in to find Kevin swinging from a blanket hooked to the doorframe. But he'd moved fast. Because he was big and Kevin was essentially a lightweight he'd been able to take the man's full weight while he'd roared for his wife to come through from the residence. Helga had stood on a chair and had managed to unhook Kevin while her husband kept Kevin's weight from his neck, and then the policeman had started mouth-to-mouth resuscitation.

By the time Darcy had arrived, Kevin was starting to breathe again.

Kevin had been lucky. The blanket had been soft and hadn't cut into his throat. He hadn't snapped a vertebra as many hanging suicides did.

He'd live.

But he'd taken some work. The man was distraught—totally bereft—and Darcy had finally stopped trying to comfort him. He'd administered sedatives and made the decision to transfer him to hospital.

'I didn't want him here in the first place,' the sergeant admitted. 'There's warrants for his boss's arrest but nothing on this guy. I just kept him for the night because he wanted to stay close to his boss, and I thought I might take the heat off the refuge.'

'But you worried enough to listen out for him.'

'He seemed desperate when we brought them in,' the policeman told him. 'He kept telling Hatfield that he'd stick with him but the last time he did... We were about to put them into a cell together when Kevin put a hand on Hatfield's shoulder and Hatfield turned round and kicked him. Like a stray dog. Worse. He kicked him so hard that I could add an assault charge to whatever else that bastard's up for. So I put them in separate cells and then I thought I'd read my book out here tonight rather than go back and sit with Helga. Cliff's on night duty so I was going to have him come in when I went to bed.'

He was a great cop, Darcy thought again. To recognise desperation...

He spent a little time with the sergeant and his wife before he left, talking through what had happened as Kevin drifted into sleep. Doing a debrief. It was the least they deserved. Finally he'd left, loading Kevin into the ambulance and following him to hospital.

To be met by the next episode of the night's drama.

'Marilyn's arrested?' Leonie hadn't got the words out before he was striding down the corridor, expecting chaos. Or worse.

But it wasn't chaos, he admitted as he finally got the story from Paul. It was just unbelievable. He examined Marilyn and found her deeply asleep, and if he hadn't had two nurses corroborating each other's stories he would never have believed what had happened.

'Ally did this? Ally got her back from cardiac arrest?'

'She's good,' Paul said seriously. 'She's a bloody fine doctor. Hell, Darcy, we didn't even have the monitor attached.'

'Why not?'

'Marilyn must have unplugged it,' Paul told him. 'She complained it made a buzz and we told her you'd ordered it to stay on. But when I went to supper and Leonie went to the bathroom, she must have decided to pull it out. That's what we think must have happened—she leaned over to un-plug it and the effort brought on the attack.'

Hell. Darcy sighed in exasperation and raked his fingers through hair that was already crazily un-ruly. It had been raked quite a few times today already. Some people were their own worst ene-mies.

'She'll have to agree to bypass surgery now,' he muttered, looking down at the sleeping woman with something akin to despair.

'Maybe she will.' Paul was looking at him, con-sidering. 'But…about Ally. Did you know Dr Westruther was a doctor?'

'It's written on her sign.'

'Yeah, but a real doctor.'

'She can't be a real doctor. Not a doctor of med-icine.'

'She must be,' Paul told him. 'Hell, Darcy, we panicked. I couldn't even get the monitor working to see if it was her heart or not, and Leonie was doing the hand-wringing she always does in a crisis. I tell you, if Ally hadn't come, we'd be wheeling Marilyn into the morgue. She knew everything. She knew exactly what to do—the right dosages, everything. And the way she did it... She's done it before, Darcy. Lots of times.'

'It doesn't make sense. And where is she now?'

'Sloped off home?' Paul suggested. He shrugged. 'Maybe if she's unregistered, she's afraid you'll sue.'

'As if I would—for saving Marilyn's life.'

'Will you go find her?'

That was what he wanted to do. Desperately. But medical imperatives ruled—as always.

'How can I?' he asked helplessly. 'I have two patients I need to settle. I need to admit Kevin. I need to organise for Marilyn's transfer first thing tomorrow—she's having her bypass whether she wants it or not, and if I organise it before she wakes then she can't argue. I'll telephone her daughter now and talk her through the options. It's going to take time.'

'Time that you'd much rather spend going round to talk to Ally?' Paul suggested, with just a hint

of mischief in his eyes, and Darcy threw him a
dark look.

'Yeah, right.'

So he worked on, in confusion.

By the time he'd finished it was almost three.
Much too late to visit Ally. Though he just happened to drive past. Well, he had to move his car
into the garage for the night, so he may as well do
a quick drive down the main street and see if her
premises were in darkness.

They were.

Finally he lay in bed in even deeper confusion.
There were so many questions.

Had she been a doctor? Was she unregistered?
Struck off for something like drug use? After all,
she was into alternative therapies.

Great. Why was he determined to paint her so
black? 'She'd throw another paintpot at me if she
could hear me thinking like this,' he told Jekyll,
who was snoring on the end of his bed. 'Maybe
I'd deserve it.'

His dog opened a bleary eye, wagged his tail
and went back to sleep. Under his bed, Hyde kept
right on snoring.

'You guys are asleep. I should be, too.

'It's not going to happen.

'So?'

'So if Ally doesn't want to be a doctor then maybe I shouldn't ask any questions?' He was discussing it with the dogs.

They weren't answering.

'I shouldn't ask Ally.

'Of course I'll ask Ally.' It was as much as he could do not to get out of bed and ask questions right then.

He didn't. But it was only because he knew very well that at three in the morning there'd be no answers. But the moment morning came those questions were going to be answered.

CHAPTER SIX

UNLIKE Darcy, when Ally hit the pillow she went out like a light. She was exhausted past belief, and although she'd thought the trauma of the day would keep her staring at the ceiling it did no such thing.

She'd saved Marilyn's life.

The thought was like some sort of heat bag that she could hug, warming parts of her she hadn't known were cold. It took away the awfulness of the day, the horror of facing Jerry. The pain.

And Jerry was in jail. She hadn't been able to stop him all those years ago but now he'd spend years behind bars. All the people whose lives he'd messed with in the past would read about it in the newspapers and say to themselves, He's a convicted felon. He's of no worth.

And if he was of no worth then the fact that he'd indoctrinated the same belief into them could somehow—please?—be assuaged.

It was a fine thought. It let her relax into her pillows with a sigh of contentment, and that was her last thought for a very long time.

* * *

She woke to banging.

Urgent banging.

She opened one eye and glanced cautiously at her bedside clock. Eight-fifteen.

This was her first morning of being open for business, she thought with a little glow of anticipation. She had a sign on the door saying she was ready for clients from nine a.m. Maybe this was the first one.

Maybe that was wishful thinking. Surely a potential client wouldn't be banging with such urgency when it was three quarters of an hour before her advertised opening.

The sun was streaming in the window through the crimson oak leaves. She refused to be apprehensive on a morning like this, she told herself. She tossed back her covers, padded over to the window in her oversized T-shirt and threw open the window. Darcy was right below. He had his arms full of parcels, there were two dogs at his heels and he was banging on her door like he was really, really impatient.

'I'm not open until nine,' she said cautiously. 'If you want a massage, you need to come back.'

He stood back and looked up.

'It's about time. I've been thumping on your door for five minutes.'

'I was asleep.' She let indignation enter her voice. He unsettled her but she wasn't about to let him know that.

'Let me in.'

'I'm not dressed.'

'I have breakfast,' he said, and she thought about it. And glanced across to her bench where a solitary tea bag mocked her.

'Breakfast?'

'Eggs. Bacon. Tomatoes, crumpets, butter, orange juice, bananas, coffee, milk…'

'Enough.' There was a part of her—a really big part of her—that was saying, *Stay away from this man.* He disconcerted her and, more, he represented a world she no longer wanted anything to do with. But he was looking up with an expression that was a strange mix of hope and happiness.

He looked great. He'd lost his tie—his shirt was open and his trousers were more casual than the ones she'd seen him in until now. His hair was sort of tousled and soft.

He was smiling.

The feeling she'd gone to sleep with—that God was in his heaven and all was right with her world—was a sensation she'd hardly ever felt. Now here was this man and his face said he was feeling exactly the same. And he made the sensation grow.

Then there was the fact that his dogs were looking up at her, too, their huge eyes just as hopeful as their master's. If she locked him out, she wouldn't get a chance to hug his dogs.

She really needed her own dog. But meanwhile...

'OK,' she told him, trying to make her voice sound grudging. 'Give me five minutes to get dressed.'

'One minute,' he told her. 'Otherwise the boys and I will start on the bacon.'

'Three minutes. Don't you dare.'

She moved.

This was her opening day, she reminded herself as she had the world's fastest shower and hauled on jeans and T-shirt. She'd change for work later.

From one lot of faded clothes to another?

So what? Her bubble of happiness refused to be dissolved because of worry that she didn't have the right outfit. Today was her first day of being a professional massage therapist, and she'd enjoy it. As she'd enjoy hugging Jekyll and Hyde. And eating breakfast with their master?

Enough. Don't ask questions, she told her reflection. She dragged a comb though her hair, took a disparaging look at herself in the cracked mirror over the bathroom basin, stuck out her tongue—and went to let in breakfast.

She smiled as she swung the door wide. He smiled, too, but then his smile faded.

She took an involuntary step backward.

'What?' she said, a trifle breathlessly.

'You're a doctor.'

It was like a slap. Oh, let's get right to the point, she thought.

'Did you smile at me just so I'd let you in?' she demanded, and he looked confused.

'No, I…'

'Then smile again, or I'm not letting you in. Breakfast or not. This is a gorgeous morning and I refuse to let you spoil it.' She glowered her best glower, and then she sighed as his smile didn't return. He was looking as if he didn't have a clue who or what she was.

Well, maybe she had to face this some time. She'd asked for it. And turning away Jekyll and Hyde would be just plain cruel. 'OK, forget the inquisition and bring in the bacon,' she told him. 'Or are you just dropping it off and running?'

'I'm here to share.'

'Then come in. But you have to be nice.'

'Of course I'll be nice.'

'You don't be nice by saying ''You're a doctor'' as if you're saying ''You're a particularly poisonous and unwashed scorpion''.'

It didn't produce so much as a glimmer of a smile. 'Why didn't you tell me?'

'I did,' she said in some indignation. 'In fact, in case you hadn't noticed, I painted the fact in letters six feet high right next to the place you work. *Dr Westruther*. Bright blue paint. I seem to remember that you noticed.'

'I didn't mean…'

Her glower deepened. She took the parcels from his arms and marched up the stairs without looking back. 'Come on, guys,' she said to Jekyll and Hyde. 'Your master's being thick. Come help me cook while we wait for him to come to his senses. I hope he's brought some for you, too.'

She didn't speak to him again. She marched over to her cooker and busied herself hauling out pans and toaster and plates, then started to cook bacon—of which there was an entirely satisfactory amount. She was aware of him watching her in silence, as if he didn't have a clue what she was.

Great. She had him nicely off balance. That was how it should be, and long might it last. The fact that she was thoroughly disconcerted as well had to be ignored.

'I looked at the Medical Board web-site,' he told her at last. 'At six this morning.'

She focussed on her bacon. 'Gee,' she said dryly. 'How fascinating. I thought about it. At six a.m. I remember thinking, Will I wake up and look on the Medical Board web-site? Or will I sleep for another couple of hours? Hard choice.'

She knew he still wasn't smiling. But there was no way she was looking.

'You're listed as a doctor.'

She sighed. 'How about that?'

'You're registered.'

'Most doctors are.'

'Your qualifications are on the site. When I found your name, I rang a friend who organises the internships from your university. He said not only did you do brilliantly at university, you've also done the first part of obstetric training. You passed with flying colours.'

'My, you have been busy. Did your friend thank you for ringing him at six a.m.?'

'Ally, will you look at me?'

'I'm cooking bacon.'

There was an exasperated sigh. 'For heaven's sake...'

'For heaven's sake what?'

'If you're a qualified doctor with brilliant obstetric training, what the hell are you doing in a dump like this?'

Then she turned. She stood with her back to the stove and surveyed what he would be seeing. Her little apartment consisted of one room. The floor was bare linoleum, with a few cracks and holes. A mattress on the floor was her bed. She hadn't pulled up the blankets. Unmade bed was bad, she thought ruefully. Never entertain visitors with an unmade bed. But, then, he had brought breakfast.

What else? She had a folding table, one upright chair and one ancient squishy chair hauled over to the window so she could read in good light. There was a dingy little bathroom leading off at the back and that was all.

Home.

But this room was a means to an end. Eventually it'd be another massage area. If things worked out.

Meanwhile… 'Are you saying my apartment is a dump?' she asked, her voice dangerous. 'Or is it this town you're describing? Either way you're out of line.'

He shook his head in disbelief. 'What on earth have you done with your salary for the last six years? And why aren't you practising as a doctor?'

The dogs were nosing around her ankles. She bent and hugged them, buying herself time to consider.

'I spend my money on wild living,' she said at last. 'And what I do is my choice.'

'My friend, Steven, said you were top of your year. He said you're one of the best doctors he ever trained. And there's no blemish against you. No lawsuit.'

'Oh, of course,' she said cordially. 'Go straight to the obvious. That I must have been drummed out of medicine with a lawsuit.'

'I didn't think that,' he told her. 'Last night Paul said you were the best doctor he's ever seen. Marilyn owes her life to you.'

'How is she?' Ally was still hugging dogs but her voice was suddenly anxious. In truth, she'd hated leaving last night. It had been panic that had driven her away. She hadn't been ready to face questions that she still wasn't ready to face now. But Marilyn...

'She's good. No, she's great. We've organised an air ambulance to take her to Melbourne at midday. Her daughter, Sue, is driving here now to accompany her. With the bypass surgery she's finally agreed to, her prognosis is excellent. Thanks to you.'

'G-good.' She continued to concentrate on the dogs. 'And Kevin?'

'Kevin has a really bruised throat but he'll survive. I have him on oxygen and sedatives. He's going to take a lot of counselling.'

'They all will.' She hesitated but she needed to ask. 'And the kids?'

'I think Jody's turned the corner. She sat up this morning and drank a little lemonade. And the other two are fine. I've let their mothers take them back to the refuge.'

'Good.' She faltered. 'Great.'

'The bacon's burning.'

She looked up at him then, her eyes meeting his. Locking.

It was a strange moment. A harsh moment. The dogs were nuzzling her, investigating her jeans and her shoes, and her hands were fondling their ears. But she was caught. By Darcy. He was staring down at her as if he was seeing something he'd never seen before—and she couldn't tear her eyes away.

The bacon spat, a great hissing splat that had the dogs looking up in hopeful expectation of a rasher zooming downward. It broke the moment, but still... As she rose to attend to her cooking, he reached forward to turn the gas ring down and she brushed his body and...

And nothing, she told herself fiercely. And nothing at all. How could brushing against someone cause something that was almost an electric jolt?

This was ridiculous.

'How many eggs?' she asked, a trifle breathlessly, and somehow she regrouped and forced her voice into neutral. 'I'm...I'm having two.'

'Of course you are,' he agreed, taking the egg container. Their fingers brushed. Damn, there it went again. That frisson of inexplicable sensation. 'I'll do that. You need to put the crumpets in the toaster.'

'I know.' She turned away with relief. What on earth was happening?

Concentrate on breakfast.

She waited until the crumpets popped up, buttered them, placed them on plates and turned to let him load them with eggs and bacon.

Still that tension.

'Did Jerry starve you?' he asked curiously, and she gave him a reluctant smile.

'Jerry hasn't been in the position of being able to do anything to me for seventeen years.'

'So you starve yourself?'

'No,' she told him.

'Then why isn't your fridge full?'

'I have other things to do with my money.'

'Other things than eat?'

'Leave it alone.' She took her plate and stalked across to the armchair by the window, and the dogs came to sit adoringly at her feet. 'Ask your master for some, guys,' she told them. She turned to their master. 'You can have the chair and the table.'

'Gee, thanks.'

'It's the least I can do when someone brings me my breakfast.' Then she addressed herself to her food, studiously not looking at him. She had no idea why he had the effect on her that he did. She didn't understand and she wasn't sure that she wanted to.

Darcy loaded his own plate. He looked across at her for a long moment but she kept right on eating. Regardless. Finally he did, too.

The silence continued. Then he set his plate aside. 'Ally?'

'Yes?'

Mistake. She shouldn't have given him an opening, she thought. But she had and he took it.

'Ally, I need to know—'

'You need to know nothing.'

'You're a qualified doctor.'

'See, you know already.'

'But I need—'

'What?' She flashed him an irritated glance. 'What do you need?'

'Help,' he said flatly. 'You know that. This place is impossible for one doctor.'

'My grandfather managed it. You can manage it.'

'The population around here is ten times what it was when your grandfather worked here. I can't cope. People die because I can't be everywhere at once.'

She glared at that. 'Don't blackmail me.'

'I'm not blackmailing you. But I need to understand—'

'You don't need to understand anything. I'm not a doctor.'

'Then why are you paying registration fees?'

Good question. She bit her lip. That was the final step, but until now...

It wasn't going to make a difference, she told herself miserably. She'd gone through it. She'd made her decision. Whatever she did could make no difference now.

'Look, Darcy, breakfast was great,' she told him. 'But yesterday I had no business to interfere with Marilyn.'

'You saved her life.'

'Yeah, and it felt good,' she admitted. 'So I can't say I'm sorry. But I don't want any part of it. Not any more. I'm no longer a doctor.'

'You are.'

'I'm not,' she said flatly.

'Why on earth not?'

'That's none of your business.'

'If I can just use you for back-up—'

'You can't.' She shrugged. 'This is stupid. I'm not a practising doctor any more. I'm a massage therapist. If someone stopped being a train driver and started being a florist, no one would ask them to do a little train driving on the side.'

'In an emergency they would. If the train was stuck.'

'Maybe for the first six months. When they still had the skills.'

'You still have the skills.'

'They'll fade. I won't keep them up.' She took a deep breath. She'd made this decision and she had to see it to its logical conclusion. 'Darcy, like it or not, I'm immovable on this. I've changed. I do a great massage. I can make people feel good. I love my new job.'

'But there's no need—'

'For people to feel good? You're telling me that the massage I gave to Lorraine last night wasn't effective? And Gloria? No one's touched her since her husband died. I bet she went to bed last night and slept like a baby. I love what I do, Darcy Rochester. It's what I am. It's who I am.'

'You're a doctor.'

'I'm a masseuse.'

'You're hiding.'

'And you're not?'

He paused. 'What do you mean by that?'

'You're not running from the tragedy of your wife's death?'

He stared. 'What the hell…?'

'You can't run from the past.'

There was a moment's silence while he thought about that. 'Is that why you came back here, then?' His voice was almost a whisper. His tone was that of discovery. Like he'd discovered the truth. 'You came back to face the past?'

Ouch. It was so close to the truth that it made her flinch. But she wasn't about to give this man the upper hand.

'If I'm doing that then it's more than you're doing.'

'You know nothing about it,' he told her. 'Rachel and I—'

'I don't need to hear.'

'You do, you know,' he told her, and his voice became even more gentle. 'You accused me of running when nothing could be further from the truth. Rachel and I had a wonderful relationship. A wonderful marriage.'

'I don't—'

'We met in high school,' he told her, ignoring her interruption. 'We were best of friends. We started med school together and then Rachel was diagnosed with leukaemia. We went through five years of treatment and remission and treatment and remission and finally we faced her death. Together.'

'I'm…I'm sorry.'

'But the thing is,' he said, his voice suddenly relentless, 'that I kcpt faith with our dream. We'd always wanted to practise in the country. Always. With Rachel's illness it wasn't possible, but we used to escape every chance we had and drive through remote little hamlets, figuring out where our ideal practise would be as soon as Rachel got better.'

'I—'

'But she didn't get better,' he told her, his voice flat, almost ruthless. 'Six months after she died, though, I came back to the town we'd decided was the perfect place to work. Here. So how the hell you think I'm running away…'

So much for a perfect day. She was feeling about three inches tall.

'So I'm not hiding,' he told her. 'But you…'

'I'm not.'

'You're running from medicine.'

'No!'

'Then why—?'

'Leave it.'

'I'm damned if I will. Not without a reason. Ally, this town doesn't need a massage therapist. It's desperate for a doctor.'

'It has you.'

'We could work together. There's plenty of work for us both to make a living.'

'Why would I want to work with you?' she demanded in desperation. 'You just keep shouting at me.'

Silence. Stalemate. He was staring at her in baffled frustration.

More silence.

'You know, you won't make a living,' he said at last. 'No one will come.'

'They might.'

'Maybe one or two.'

'In five minutes,' she said, glancing at her watch, 'I'm opening my front door as a massage therapist. I'd imagine in five minutes you'll be starting work as you always do next door. We're professional colleagues but in different professions. Now, if you'll excuse me…'

'I won't excuse you.'

But it seemed he had no choice. There was a shout from below. A woman's voice.

'Ally. Ally Westruther. You're wanted down here. Now!'

Silence.

'Ally,' the voice called again, and Ally smirked.

'This'll be my first customer,' she told him, and he raised his brows in disbelief.

'You wish.'

'Yeah, and you just wish I'd go away.'

'Of course I don't. But if you're going to advertise that you're a doctor...'

'Ally!'

'It's Betty,' Darcy snapped. 'My receptionist. So much for your first customer.' He gave Ally a last frustrated glance and strode to the still open window.

'I'm here,' he called—and then he stopped.

Ally peered over his shoulder.

It wasn't just Betty.

Half the population of Tambrine Creek seemed to be assembled out on the main street. People waving balloons, banners, placards. People holding plates of food. Guys with crates of what looked like glasses, and more crates with bottles of...champagne?

'Darcy.' Betty was standing on Ally's front step, holding a huge tray of sandwiches. 'What are you doing up here?'

'Um...visiting,' he said weakly, and Ally was pushing him aside and shoving her head out the window.

'Betty,' she said in astounded delight, and she leaned so far that Darcy caught hold of her and held on. She leaned further and he was forced to hold tighter.

'Hey,' she said, her face breaking into a huge smile as she saw the extent of the congregation assembled in her street. The balloons. The placards. 'It's a party.'

'It surely is,' Betty told her. 'Read the placards. Hush, everyone.' She turned and waved and the crowd fell silent. They must have been under instruction, Ally thought, stunned. There'd been absolute silence until Betty had called out, but as Ally appeared there was a swelling murmur of speculation.

Doctor caught in bedroom of massage therapist. Whoops.

But Betty was in charge and speculation wasn't on the agenda. She handed her sandwich tray to someone and braced in speech position.

'Ladies and gentlemen,' she said, and someone at the back gave a derisory hoot.

'Yeah, and the rest of us. Get on with it, Betty.'

'I just want to say something about Ally.'

'Say it.'

Betty grinned. She smiled up at Ally, her broad, kind face taking in the fact that Darcy was leaning out as well.

'Ally's come back,' she said, turning to the crowd again. 'Our Ally. We hated seeing her go all those years ago and we're delighted she's back. We love the fact that she's setting up in this town and we're tickled pink that there's a Dr Westruther in town again.' Her beam widened still more and she motioned to the mass of banners.

WELCOME ALLY, the sign said.

And...

MASSAGE ROCKS, said another.

And...

WE LOVE DR WESTRUTHER, said a third.

'This morning Ally thought she was opening for business without fanfare,' Betty told them. 'But when any business opens there should be a ceremony and when any house starts being lived in there should be a house-warming. So this is it, Ally, dear,' she said, turning again to smile up at Ally. 'We started an appointment book for you, and you're booked out solid from eleven a.m. this morning for the rest of the week. But for now...welcome to your Welcome-to-Tambrine-Creek party, Ally Westruther. Come on down.'

Nine o'clock on a Tuesday morning was a really stupid time for a street party but that was what was happening. Darcy stood on the doorstep of his surgery and gazed at the partygoers in disbelief.

Betty, he thought. It had to be Betty who'd organised this whole thing and, as if on cue, she appeared at his elbow.

'Isn't this lovely?'

'You never welcomed me like this,' he said with a grudging smile, and she smiled back.

'No, but you didn't need it. When you arrived we were overjoyed to see you, but you were still sore after Rachel's death and we knew enough to welcome you gently.'

'You knew about Rachel's death before I arrived?'

'It's a small town,' she said simply. 'Everyone knows everyone else's business, and if they don't know it they worry. That's why it was so amazing that Jerome Hatfield's been up on the ridge all this time and we didn't realise it was him.'

'So the small-town network let you down.' He gazed out to where Ally was balancing a glass of champagne in one hand, a lamington in the other, and was submitting to someone looping balloons through her earrings. 'Did you know Ally was a real doctor?'

'We haven't seen Ally for nearly twenty years. I know her dad died years back and her mother's been in and out of mental institutions.'

'Her mother's still alive?'

'As far as I know.' She hesitated. 'You know, that's one of the reasons everyone's making such a fuss. There are people who feel guilty that we should have done more to help Ally, and also her mother.'

'Why?'

'Her mother, Elizabeth, was only fifteen when she got pregnant to Ally's father,' Betty told him. 'Elizabeth's father—Ally's grandfather—was rigid with rage. He hauled her into the surgery right here and examined her and he came storming out like he was going to explode. He'd had such plans for her. She was really bright and I can remember he'd told everyone she was going to be the next town doctor. Until that day. I was a junior then, and I remember cowering back, thinking he was going to hit me. Thinking he was going to hit someone. ''Get me Saul Newitt on the phone,'' he yelled. Saul Newitt was the nearest obstetrician with a…well, with a dubious reputation. ''She's going to have an abortion right now.'' But while he was ranting Elizabeth took off. She climbed out a back window and Ally's dad must have been waiting because they disappeared.'

He flinched. Hell. Poor lonely kid. 'Did Dr Westruther try to find them?'

'Oh, of course he did,' she told him. 'But they were gone. And maybe they had reason if her father was going to force her to have an abortion. Then when the little one was about four, Elizabeth brought Ally home. You wouldn't have believed it was the same girl. All the life had gone out of her. The old man didn't help—he gave her a hard time every minute she was here—and when she disappeared again he didn't try to find her.'

'But you knew where she'd gone.'

'She told someone—Marilyn, I think—in case something happened to the old man. So when Ally's grandpa died we found her. Only it was too late. Elizabeth was really sick then.'

'Sick?'

'Just…empty,' she said. 'Ally's father came and took Ally away but Elizabeth was finished. It was written up in the newspapers when Jerry was arrested. Her mental instability. How Ally had to go into a foster home. It was a really sad story.' She sighed and then looked determinedly to where a laughing Ally was surrounded by a sea of balloons.

'But who would have thought she'd end up back here? She must have ended up with really good foster-parents. Paul's told everyone what happened last night. A qualified doctor as well as a masseuse.' She grinned and nudged him. 'You can't whinge now about her sign.'

He tried a glower to match Ally's. 'I can whinge if I want.'

'Misery.' She laughed and he was forced to smile as well. But he had to move on. 'Come and have some champagne,' she said, and he shook his head.

'I have patients booked.'

'They cancelled,' she told him. 'Everyone wanted to be at the party.'

'Great. That'll make my afternoon frantic.'

'Do you have to be a grouch?'

'I guess not.' He was still watching Ally moving among the townspeople as if they were her family. She looked...happy, he thought, and suddenly he didn't begrudge her a moment of it. Why should he?

This was nothing to do with him, he told himself. Five days ago he had been the sole doctor in this town, and nothing had changed. He had no right to try and impose a medical career on someone who didn't want it. Sure, Ally's path might be incomprehensible, but it was her path and she had the right to follow it.

It was none of his business.

It didn't make him feel any better, though. He stood and watched her and suddenly he was washed with a surge of loneliness—of longing—a feeling so strong that it matched those he'd experienced in the first awful months after Rachel died. Six long years ago.

What the hell was he thinking of? He shook himself, pushing away sensations he didn't understand.

'I'll do the house calls I couldn't fit in last night,' he told Betty, and she cast him a strange look.

'OK, but be back by eleven.'

'Why?'

'Because I've booked you from eleven,' she told him with exaggerated patience. 'We don't want to keep A—anyone waiting.'

Darcy did four house calls in two hours—all to patients who weren't far from the hospital. He couldn't go far because of Marilyn's needs.

So he saw one influenza—well, head cold really, but if Rosie Lenmon wanted to insist it was influenza, he wouldn't argue. He saw two elderly patients for routine checks and Bert Prine with quinsy. He admitted Bert to hospital, gave him intravenous antibiotics, analgesia and a lecture on not getting his affected throat seen to earlier—and then did a quick check on all his patients while he was there.

Everything was great. Marilyn was soundly asleep, which was what she desperately needed. The medical notes were written up for her transfer to Melbourne. She'd received such a fright that when she'd woken first thing this morning, she'd agreed without a single argument to whatever Darcy had suggested. Soon her daughter would arrive to accompany her on the Med-Flight-Transfer—and see she didn't change her mind.

Kevin also was asleep. He was heavily sedated. He needed psychiatric help, Darcy thought, looking down at the little man in concern. As soon as his throat settled he'd talk him through the options.

Not yet. For now, sleep was the only answer. Sleep and food and kindness.

Maybe that was the only cure.

His last concern was Jody, and Jody was asleep as well. Margaret was sitting by her daughter's bedside, eating a lamington that had been provided by the street-party revellers. When Darcy glanced around the door she looked as if she was in heaven. Darcy didn't disturb her. It'd be a cruel thing, to interrupt a woman's first association with a lamington in years.

The helicopter arrived then, landing behind the hospital, and Marilyn's daughter arrived as well. The next half-hour was busy with organising the transfer. Finally as the doctors on board took over Marilyn's care, he stood back to bid Sue the best of luck.

'I wish I had time to thank Ally,' Sue told him. 'I came as fast as I could. But I need to go with Mum. You will thank her for me?'

'Of course I will.' He hesitated. It wasn't the time or the place but... 'You knew Ally when you were kids?'

'We were best friends. She used to love coming to our place. Mum and Dad wanted to care for her when her grandpa died but then that creep of a father came to get her. Both her parents were living with that Jerry creature.' She hesitated. 'I can't believe he's turned up here after all these years. Mum rang me about him last night and I've been wondering whether the fuss pushed her into heart failure. She was so upset when Ally was put into foster care.'

'Did you keep in touch with Ally?'

She shrugged, watching the paramedics lifting her mother's stretcher into position. 'We tried,' she told him. 'The first time Jerry was arrested, Ally was put into a foster home. Mum and Dad tried to see if we could have her but Social Services insisted on keeping all the kids from the commune together.'

'Sue?'

The doctor on board was calling. Her mother was ready and Ally's problems had to be put aside. She gave Darcy a rueful smile and then hugged him. 'Thank you for giving me Mum back,' she said simply.

'Thank Ally.'

'Hug Ally for me, too,' she told him. 'She needs all the hugs she can get.'

That was the end of Darcy's medical imperatives. He walked back to his consulting rooms feeling as if he ought to be pleased, but he was vaguely uneasy. Why? The revellers had gone. He could get back to normal.

From now on he could ignore Ally, he told himself, medical qualifications or not.

She needs all the hugs she can get.

His dogs were trotting by his side. 'Maybe I'll lend her you guys,' he told them.

They wagged their tails, as if in total agreement, and he felt a stupid, irrational surge of something that surely couldn't be jealousy? Could it?

Jealous that she'd hug his dogs? He was going out of his mind.

Betty was waiting for him. She was sitting at reception and she had her arms folded, like she was guarding the entrance against unwanted intruders. She patted the dogs and pointed to their baskets, waiting until they'd obeyed the woman who was clearly more their boss than their designated master, and then she turned her attention back to Darcy.

'You're not wanted here,' she told him.

'As far as I know, this is where I'm expected to be,' he said dryly, tossing his bag into the corner and reaching for his normal pile of patient notes. They weren't there. 'It's eleven o'clock. I have appointments.'

'You have an appointment,' she corrected him. 'One appointment. Singular.'

'I'm sorry?'

'Next door.' She smiled at his look of bemusement. 'It's the town's surprise. We talked about who was going to have first go. Gloria sneaked in while no one was looking, but we decided that Ally's first real patient should be someone special. And after last night there was no question. So the town's people have clubbed together and we've paid for Ally's first massage. We've given it to you.'

He gazed at her as if he couldn't see her. 'To me,' he said stupidly.

'Now, don't you dare tell us you won't accept it,' she said, making her voice severe. Which didn't quite match her mischievous twinkle. 'Even people who could barely afford it put twenty cents toward this. It's the town's gift to both of you. An hour and a half's massage. No one's booked here until two. Off you go next door, and don't come back until you're so relaxed you're horizontal.'

'You have to be kidding.'

'I'm not kidding. Ally's waiting.'

'I'm not going to have a massage with Ally.'

'Then half the town will have their feelings hurt and Ally won't have a first client. Do you want that to happen?'

'No, but—'

'You're afraid.'

'Of course I'm not.'

'Then what are you waiting for?' she demanded. 'Do you want to be known as a stubborn, cantankerous old stick-in-the-mud who's refusing to admit that there might be some advantage in holistic remedies? Or are you going to accept this gift?'

'You don't think there might be some middle ground?' he asked cautiously, and she shook her head.

'Nope.' She grinned. 'There's not. A dozen people have decided their medical problems aren't so urgent that they can't wait until after your massage, Dr Rochester. Now, if you intend to sit here and sulk…'

'I'm not sulking.'

'No,' she told him, and rose from her desk and started to push him out the door. 'You're going next door. Ally's waiting. Off you go. Right now!'

CHAPTER SEVEN

THEY hadn't told Ally.

Stunned, Darcy was propelled by the insistent Betty up Ally's front steps and through her front door.

'Here's your first client,' Betty called up the stairs. She grinned at Darcy, then disappeared, slamming the door after her.

Ally appeared at the head of the stairs—and stopped.

'You.'

He couldn't think of a thing to say. Nothing.

'What are you doing here?'

'It seems,' he managed, almost apologetically, 'that I'm your first client.' But he was having trouble saying anything.

Until now he'd only seen Ally in jeans. She was still casually dressed, but she'd changed. She was wearing baggy, three-quarter-length trousers, an oversized sweatshirt with the sleeves rolled up, and bare feet. Her hair was twisted into a casual knot. Her freckles were subdued with a tiny application of make-up, and her lips were painted the same soft pink as her sweatshirt.

170

She looked gorgeous.

He was staring.

'What?' she said crossly, as she hauled herself together and came on down. 'Have I got a blob on my nose?'

He shook himself, trying to shed this overwhelming feeling of unreality. 'Sorry. I was staring.'

'I know you were,' she said cautiously, as if she might be humouring a lunatic. 'That's why I was asking. So if I haven't got a blob on my nose...' She sighed and gave up. 'OK. Let's not go there. But for a moment I thought you said you were my first client.'

'I am.'

She thought about it and finally she nodded. With caution. The lunatic approach obviously still had appeal.

'You're supposed to be working,' she told him.

'It appears I'm not,' he said, a shade grimly. 'My patients have organised that no one's sick for the next couple of hours.'

'Your patients?'

'The town,' he told her. 'The town has donated a massage. To me. Apparently I'm to be your first customer. What you did last night in saving Marilyn has flown round the town and everyone's fascinated. And grateful.'

'But…you…'

'They're also grateful to me,' he said, trying not to sigh. 'It's the way it is in the country. I get given things.'

'What sort of things?'

He hesitated. But the tension had to be overcome somehow. Why not try talking?

'When Rachel died I went overseas,' he told her. 'One of the airlines I flew with gave away tiny bottles of some sort of blue liqueur. The bottle caught my fancy. I started looking out for miniature bottles, and when I set up here I organised a dozen or so in a wall frame.'

'So?' she said, still with that cautious edge.

'So my patients knew I was interested in collecting little liqueur bottles,' he told her, digging his hands deep into his pockets and trying not to sound stupid. 'As of the last count I have two thousand, three hundred and twenty-five bottles, and that's not counting the ones that have come in this week.'

She gazed at him in astonishment, and her face creased into a delighted smile of recognition.

'They used to give Grandpa fish,' she told him. 'We lost count of the fishermen who couldn't afford to pay and brought fish instead. Grandpa and I had a burial ground out the back of the hospital. One day someone will dig it up and wonder what sort of ancient tribe wasted so many fish. Grandpa sneaked heaps into the hospital kitchens, but even hospital patients get sick of fish.'

He grinned.

The tension between them dissipated. A little.

'So they've given you me to massage,' he told her. 'Instead of liqueur. And instead of fish.'

The tension zoomed back.

'Um…what are we going to do?' she asked.

'I'm booked for a massage.'

'Do you want a massage?'

'No.'

'Have you ever had a massage?'

'No.'

'Then how do you know you don't want one?'

'I guess…'

'They'll ask,' she told him. 'If you were given it as a collective present, you'll be asked. Boy, were Grandpa and I grilled about our fish. Which one was the tastier? Do you like barracuda better than flathead? What are you going to say about my massage?'

'It was a very nice massage?'

'That's pathetic. You could say that about fish.'

'Then you tell me what to say.'

'Nope.' She pushed her sleeves higher with a determined little shove. 'There's only one thing to be done.'

'No.'

'If you don't,' she told him, 'then I'm going to be honest. When asked, I'll tell them that Dr Darcy Rochester was too shy to have a massage.'

'I'm not too shy.'

'Too chicken?'

'And I'm not afraid.'

'Then what? Do you disapprove of the profession so much you won't even try?'

'I don't disapprove.'

'That's what it looks like from here.' She tapped her foot. 'You know, it really doesn't hurt.'

'I...'

'And I'll bet you're tense as all get-out. I can practically see the tension from here.'

'I'm not tense!'

'Yeah, and I suppose you're raising your voice because you always raise your voice.'

'Look—'

'The way I see it,' she told him, 'is that people will be watching. The locals saw you come in this door five minutes ago and they'll expect you to leave in a little over an hour looking nicely re-laxed, as if you've had a really good massage. So the options are that you can stalk out right now, hurting people's feelings in the process. You can sit here like a dummy for an hour and a half—and I'm warning you I don't even have any magazines for you to kill time with. Or you can have a massage. Why don't you want a massage?' she asked. 'Are you scared I'll jump you?'

His eyebrows hit his hairline. 'No, I...'

'I'm a professional,' she told him. 'I'm a registered massage therapist. I can be struck off for behaving unethically, and jumping you is definitely unethical. Besides...' She grinned. 'Strange as it seems, I'm not even tempted. So are you going to accept a massage or are you going to look a gift horse in the mouth?'

'You being a gift horse?'

'That's the ticket,' she said approvingly, and tossed him a towel from the pile on the warming rack. 'I'm going upstairs. You need to undress down to your jocks, lie on the table and cover yourself with a towel. I'll come down when you're decent. Sandalwood, Dr Rochester?'

'Sandalwood?'

'For relaxation. Or something else. Check out the list on the wall before you lie down. Headaches, tension, constipation...you name it I can rub you with something that just might make you feel better.'

'Constipation?'

She grinned. 'I won't take a case history,' she

told him. 'And if you just happen to choose marigold for premenstrual tension, then I won't ask any questions at all.'

Darcy undressed. Slowly.

He was feeling really, really weird. This was a bad idea. Stupid.

He lay on her sun-warmed couch and covered himself with her pre-warmed towel. Sunbeams were filtering through the blinds. This was a lovely place for a massage, he thought. She'd known what she was about when she'd chosen her premises.

But then the reasons why she'd chosen her rooms faded, as did any other logical thought. He couldn't think of anything other than the fact that any minute Ally would walk down those stairs and begin her massage.

He tried again. This was crazy. He should be next door. If he'd known he had cancellations he could have gone out to dress old Martin Pegg's leg ulcers.

He'd let her give him a quick rub just to keep the locals happy, he decided with the frayed remnants of the senses left to him. Maybe he could go out the back way so no one would see him leaving early. OK, he couldn't take his car away, but he could catch up on some medico-legal paperwork.

Maybe…

Maybe he couldn't do this. He'd draped the towel from his waist down but the sun was streaming in over his bare back. He felt... He felt...

'Ready?' Ally's soft voice floated down the stairs.

'Yes,' he said, and it came out as a croak. He coughed. 'Um...yes.'

He was lying face down, his face pillowed by a soft, circular rim that left him clear to breathe. He heard her walk down the stairs and it was all he could do not to get up and run.

'I don't think—'

'Did you choose an oil?' A soft murmur started behind him—harps with a stream rippling in the background. Oh, for heaven's sake, how corny was this?

'Sandalwood,' he said, and his voice was desperate. He couldn't see, but he heard her smile in her response.

'How original is that? And expensive.' He could hear her smile. 'I'll have to charge you an extra dollar if you choose sandalwood.'

'Can we just get on with it?'

'Sure.' She was draping another warm towel over him, adjusting him so he was covered from neck to toe.

'Just relax,' she told him. 'Think of nothing. Sink into the music.'

Her hands came to rest on the broad stretch of his back, and through the warmth of the towel he felt a wide, soft pressure as she gently pressed down. She stayed where she was for a long, long minute, her hands simply resting. Being in contact with him.

Then, ever so gently, she lifted the towel away—the towel that covered his back from the waist up. The other—the one that covered his legs—she left in place.

'Think of nothing but the water you're hearing,' she murmured. He heard her rubbing her hands, warming the oil, he thought. Then, very lightly, her hands returned to his back. Her hands floated downward, barely touching him but sweeping down in long, curving strokes that followed the curves of his body as she spread the warmed oil over his skin.

Over and over.

Her feather touch became firmer, a broad, definite sweep that was doing more than spread the sweet-smelling oil. It warmed him to the core. It made him feel...

He didn't know how he felt.

Forget asking. Think of nothing.

The strokes became firmer still, rolling up in wide arcs from his thighs to his shoulders. Her hands circled out from the small of his back, under his arms, back to his shoulder blades, sweeping down over his shoulders, warming his neck.

'It's effleurage,' she murmured. 'Just used to warm and relax.'

It certainly did. He was feeling hazy already.

Then the long strokes stopped. Her hands rested for a moment on his back, as though considering.

Then her magic hands started work again.

'Petrissage,' she murmured, and he realised she was explaining to try and stop the tension he was feeling at the touch of her. Turning it into technical terms he could relate to.

She was working on one side, using the whole of her hands, kneading, pulling, working the mass of muscles in his broad back. Her hands weren't leaving his body between strokes—there was total contact—but she was working him as if he was warm dough.

Then the pulling... Using her entire hand from fingertip to wrist, she pulled up from his sides with alternate hands, carefully overlapping her hands at each pull, so each hand came to rest at the place where the other hand had been.

She kept explaining as she went and her voice was a soft murmur in the background, merging into the sound of the water and the music and the sensation of her hands and the sunlight on his back.

Deep tissue strokes…frictions…thumb rolling…percussion, pummelling, cupping, half-locust leg lifts…

He was close to sleep at one level, but at another he was deeply aware of every move. She rolled him over and he was hardly aware that he'd helped—that he'd moved. She was massaging his neck, and then her genius fingers were rolling in tiny circles from forehead down along his cheekbones to his jaw.

He could feel her breast against his head. He could smell her. She wasn't wearing perfume but she still smelt clean. Pure.

The sandalwood, he thought weakly. It'd be the sandalwood he was smelling.

Yeah, and it's the oil you're feeling, and not Ally, he told himself wryly but then went back to just experiencing. Just being.

Her fingers were slowing now. She left his face and he was aware of a stab of sheer regret.

Warm towels were being laid back over his body and her hands were moving lightly over him. Lightly. Lightly. Feathering. Barely brushing.

Then her hands came to rest on his chest, ever so lightly. They pressed down as if in one long gesture of farewell—and then they were gone.

The face mask she'd laid over his eyes as she'd rolled him to his back was lifted away.

He kept his eyes closed. He didn't want to break this moment.

This might be a massage—well, of course it was a massage, that was all it was—but at another level...

He'd released something he hadn't known he'd been holding, he thought, dazed. In these last few minutes his head felt as if it had been lifted from his shoulders. The tension was gone.

And what a tension. It was a tension he'd held since Rachel had died, he thought, dazed beyond belief. He felt...free.

Was that massage? Just massage?

'I'm going upstairs,' Ally whispered, and he fought to bring himself back to reality. 'Lie still for a few more minutes while you fully wake up, and then get dressed. I'll come back down a few minutes after I hear you moving round.'

He thought about that and didn't like it.

'Stay.'

'I have other clients,' she told him, and he could hear the smile back in her voice. 'And maybe so have you.'

'Didn't they book you for an hour and a half?'

'You've been here for an hour and forty minutes,' she told him, and that woke him right up. His eyes flashed open and she was laughing down at him.

He stared upward.

Her eyes were dancing. Her hair had fallen forward. She looked flushed from the exertion of the massage, flushed and happy and ready to move on.

She looked…beautiful.

'Ally…'

'I have to go,' she whispered, and her smile slipped. She took an involuntary step back. 'I…I…'

Her eyes were locked on his.

Ally.

He didn't say it. He just thought it. Ally, Ally, Ally.

It was like a shout in his head. A release. A flood of pure sweeping joy that had nothing to do with the massage. Or maybe everything.

'Ally,' he said again, and this time his voice was more urgent.

'I need to go,' she told him, and took another step backward.

'It can't be an hour and a half,' he said, and looked up at the clock over the door.

And blinked.

An hour and forty minutes, she'd said. How could that have happened?

'I'll see you when you're dressed,' she said—and fled.

He didn't blame her. Things were entirely out of control. Maybe he should run, too.

Hell, no. Not feeling like this.

It was like a huge black weight had been lifted from his chest and he hadn't known it was there.

In the last few years he'd worked through the grief of Rachel's death. He'd moved on. Or he'd thought he'd moved on. He was aware that he was lonely but he was too damned busy to do anything about it. Anyway, comparing anyone to Rachel was impossible.

But he wasn't comparing Ally to Rachel. There was no comparison. They were two different women.

Two different...loves?

He lay there with the sunlight dappling over him. He heard Ally running a sink full of water upstairs—getting rid of the oil on her hands. Preparing herself for the next client.

He had patients waiting.

Amazing as this new sensation was, it'd have to wait. He rose from the massage table and once again felt that sweep of unreality. That a massage could do so much...

Ally was right in calling this a remedial massage. Working through this extraordinary sensation would take adjustment, but even making allowances for his personal sensations he knew what she was offering had huge value. If Ally could take a client out of the problems of the present...

Claire Manning. Claire's husband had prostate cancer and was fading slowly with as much agony to those around him as he could manage. Claire loved Doug with all her heart, but she had four children under twelve and she worked full time to try and keep the family afloat. The demands Doug was making on her were driving her to the point of collapse. Doug could well live for years but in a sense he'd buried himself already. He lay in front of the television and demanded and demanded and demanded.

Claire was coming here, Darcy decided as he hauled on his boots. If he had to drag her. Once a week.

How could she fund it?

The Rotary Club, he thought. The local service club had been aching to do something for Claire. Maybe he could suggest they donate three or four massages a week and he could use them to refer people who needed them.

Bob Proody.

There was another one. Bob had copped polio when he was ten. Now in his seventies, he was so stiff he could barely manage on two sticks. His wife was dead and his only daughter was in Canada. To have a rub like this once a week...to have his aching muscles eased and to have human contact...

It was like being given access to a new wonder drug, he thought, his feeling of excitement intensifying. Then he heard footsteps on the stairs and he turned to find Ally smiling at him.

'All done?'

'I'm done,' he told her, rising and trying to keep his composure. She looked... Damn, she looked...

He was all at sea, he admitted to himself. For the last few years he'd been self-contained, calm and aloof—a spectator on other people's lives. And suddenly he was into territory he didn't recognise.

'What do I owe you?' he asked, and he didn't recognise his voice.

'It's all paid for. I thought you knew that.'

'What, even the sandalwood?'

'The town paid for sandalwood. The best is what they ordered. They think a lot of you, Darcy.'

'Yeah, well...' Damn, he was trying not to blush. 'They'll think a lot of you, too.'

'You liked your massage?'

'Um...yeah.'

'You've really never had a massage?' she asked curiously, and he shook his head.

'No.'

'It wasn't too unpleasant?'

'You could say that.' He hesitated. 'Ally, if that's how you make everyone feel…'

'I didn't do anything special to you.'

Like hell she hadn't. He gazed at her and wondered if she had any idea at all what his emotions were doing.

Medicine. Concentrate on patients.

'There are people in this town who this could really help,' he told her, and she raised her brows in disbelief.

'Yeah? But I'm the one who's here to rip people off,' she reminded him. 'Pretending to be a doctor and ripping off the life savings of people like Ivy.'

'I was out of line,' he growled. 'Can we forget it?'

She put her head on one side and thought about it. And then she smiled again. Hell, that smile… It made his gut clench.

'Ally.'

'Hmm?' She glanced at her watch and then at the door. It was time for him to leave, he thought. But…

'Ally, can we start again?' he asked. 'I've said some pretty unspeakable things to you.'

'Basket weaving,' she said thoughtfully. 'Yeah, you have.'

'Let me take you out to dinner.'

Silence.

'You don't want to do that.'

'I do.'

'Nope.' She crossed and pulled the door wide. 'Sorry.'

'What do you mean, nope?'

Her smile widened. 'Sorry, Darcy. But you're a doctor. You know as well as I do that dating patients is out of the question.'

'Dating patients?'

'I've just given you the best massage I know how to give,' she said gently, taking pity on his look of confusion. 'You're feeling warm and soporific and like everything's right with your world. Like you giving a patient a shot of pethidine. Would you give a patient a mind-altering drug and then try to date her?'

'Of course I wouldn't.'

'There you go, then,' she said cordially. 'I'm sorry, Darcy, but I do need to move on. If you'll excuse me.'

'Hell, Ally, the way I'm feeling...'

'You're feeling pretty good,' she agreed. 'And I've done that for you. Well done me. Now, off you go and see your patients and I'll see mine. If you want another massage at any time, then of course you're free to make an appointment.'

'I don't want another massage.'

'Really?'

'Ally…' He took a step toward her and she moved so she was halfway out the door. It was a practised technique, he saw suddenly. She gave massages in the main street during business hours, and if a patient made a threatening move toward her she only had to step outside. And here she was, stepping outside.

'I am not threatening you,' he told her.

'No,' she said encouragingly. 'You're not. But I have another patient booked in ten minutes and I need to clean the room. Can you leave?'

He was making a fool of himself. He took a deep breath. In the last hour and a half his world had tilted and he had no clear idea how to straighten it.

Get out of here and think about it, he told himself. Get away from her smile. From the feel of her. The scent of her.

Help.

Deep breath here.

'I'm sorry.' He managed a rueful smile and stepped out, into the day. Breaking the forced intimacy of the little sunlit room. He walked down the steps and then turned to look back at her.

'That was an inappropriate time to ask,' he told her. 'Stupid. But this massage was a one-off. From now on we're professional colleagues.'

'Are we?'

'Of course we are. And there's lots of professional issues we need to talk over.'

'I'm not practising medicine.'

'I might need to rethink my position that massage isn't medicine,' he told her. 'I can think of at least a dozen people in the district who could really benefit from this, and there's many, many more who'll love it.'

She raised her brows as if she was politely incredulous.

'Come out with me tonight and talk about it,' he urged, but her look of polite incredulity didn't change.

'I don't date clients.'

'Ally—'

'Thank you for coming,' she said, and her smile was rigidly formal. It was strained, he thought, and decided that maybe she wasn't as much in control as she made out to be. But their conversation was over.

'Good afternoon,' she told him, in a voice that was as rigidly impersonal as that of a receptionist in any mainstream medical centre.

'I need to check your foot.'

'My foot's fine.'

And before he could respond, she'd retreated, closing the door behind her.

'Hey, Doc...'

There was a call from next door. He turned to find Harold Pipping waving to him from the door of his own consulting room.

'Hey, Doc, I gotta appointment at two but I came early,' the old fisherman told him. 'I thought... I got an ingrown toenail and I figured if I came early you might have time to cut it off.'

CHAPTER EIGHT

How was a girl supposed to go back to work after that?

Thankfully, Ally's training had been comprehensive and thorough—so thorough that she was able to turn herself onto autopilot without much trouble. Thankfully also, the four massages that had been booked for the afternoon were all for healthy adults. The head of the Rotary Club, Fred, was first in line. Then his wife, Myrtle. Following on was Elaine, the local pharmacist—who closed her pharmacy for an hour to get her massage—and finally Hilda, the head teacher of the local primary school, who came at the end of her day's teaching.

She was being assessed, Ally decided as she petrissaged Hilda's leathery skin. These four were a representative sample of the town's elders, and she knew that if she made them happy it was tantamount to having a certificate saying, 'Dr Ally is respectable.'

She was incredibly grateful, but as she eased their knots of tension, warmed their muscles and made them relax so deeply that sleep that night was almost assured, her mind kept wandering to Darcy.

To the feel of him. To his smile. To the look of confusion in his eyes as he'd asked her out and she'd refused.

He'd looked confused.

Did he realise what he did to her? she wondered. And decided he couldn't. He mustn't. She was here with a goal, and that goal certainly didn't involve the local doctor. To give up all she'd given up, and then calmly walk into a relationship with a doctor who practised medicine in this town— who lived in her grandfather's house... No.

Should she have even come back here? Who knew? But as she bade an effusive Hilda goodbye, having first booked her another appointment for the same time next week, she knew the reception she was getting was mostly because of her background. People were eager to help, and they'd be eager to help her mother as well.

She bit her lip. How long?

Maybe not so long. She counted her takings and thought maybe it wouldn't be very long at all before she could rent somewhere decent and hire someone during the day for the times when her mother couldn't be alone.

She walked upstairs, conscious of the fact that she was bone weary. Five long massages in an afternoon was probably one too many, but the thought of how much she'd earned more than made up for aching muscles.

At least she had food. The revellers of the morning had left plates of leftovers. Betty had offered to throw them out and Ally had said—with dignity—that she'd dispose of them herself.

Which was just what she was doing, she thought, collapsing into her window chair and wrapping herself around a cold sausage roll. It wasn't great but it was food and it was free.

The phone rang.

'Go away,' she told it, but it kept ringing. Maybe it was someone wanting an appointment so she heaved herself out of her chair—with a groan—and answered.

'Ally.'

'Darcy.' She was straight into defence mode and he heard it.

'There's no need to put up the armour.'

'Isn't there?'

'No. I saw your light go out downstairs.'

'It happens,' she said cautiously. 'At the end of the day I turn my light off. I bet you do, too.'

'So, have you rethought dinner?'

She eyed the receiver. She eyed her sausage roll—and took another bite. Three fast chews and it was down.

'I've eaten,' she told him.

'You've eaten dinner?'

'Yep.'

'Your light only went out three minutes ago.'

'I'm a fast eater. Good night, Darcy.'

'This is crazy. There's a great little place around the headland—part of the Nautilus Resort. They have a five-star menu.'

She eyed another congealed sausage roll. 'I'm eating five-star food right now.'

'You're kidding.'

'Nope. I'm eating premium beef in a crisp wrap of melt-in-the-mouth pastry.' She looked at the ketchup container in the middle of the plate where sausage rolls had been dunked this morning. The sauce had bits of broken sausage roll floating in its murky depths.

She lifted another roll and dunked.

'With gourmet sauce on the side,' she told him. 'It's magnificent.'

'You cooked that in three minutes?'

'Not only am I the world's best masseuse,' she said modestly, 'but I cook a mean five-star dinner.'

'Want to share?'

'Cook your own.'

'I shared mine last night.'

Enough. This was getting way too familiar for comfort. And way too…enticing?

'Leave it, Darcy,' she told him. 'I don't want to take this relationship any further than the professional.'

'Professional colleagues share meals.'

'Not these two,' she told him, and put down the phone before he could say another word. She crossed back to the window and looked out—just to see if the lights were on in the surgery next door. They weren't. But Darcy was leaning against his car. He had his cell phone in his hand and he was looking up at her window.

When he saw her he smiled.

She hauled down the blind like he was as assassin. Drat the man, what was he doing?

He was unequalising her equilibrium, she told herself crossly. She had her future mapped and it was going to work. It had to work. Without Darcy.

'Have another gourmet beef roll in crispy pastry with *fine jus* on the side,' she told herself crossly. She dunked her cold sausage roll in ketchup again, slid down onto her bed and decided she'd sulk for the rest of the night. There was nothing else to do.

Sulking was all very well, but it wasn't exactly time-consuming.

For the last few nights—ever since she'd arrived in town—Ally had worked feverishly to get her rooms in order. Now her rooms were in order.

What was left to do?

She should have gone to the library and found herself a book, she thought. Where was television when you needed it?

She had three massage manuals and nothing else.

Massage manuals palled after a while.

Darcy must be long gone. She risked another glance out the window. His car was no longer there. His surgery was in darkness.

Good. Great.

It was eight at night. She could just…

What? Go to the pub?

She could go down to the refuge, she thought suddenly. She hadn't seen any of the commune people all day. They'd be totally disorientated. For years they'd have been doing exactly what Jerry ordered, and now the future was theirs to do with as they wished. The concept would be terrifying.

Maybe it wouldn't hurt to see whether any of them would like a gentle shoulder and neck massage before they slept. Maybe she could even talk to them about Jerry.

It wasn't her business, she told herself, but, then, it was she who'd pulled the rug from under them. She'd been the catalyst in Jerry's arrest.

Jerry was still in town. She'd spoken briefly to the police sergeant that morning. With outstanding warrants in three Australian states, plus one out-standing warrant in the U.S., there was some dis-cussion as to where to take him. It had been de-cided he was to stay in Tambrine Creek until it was sorted.

For the people in the refuge, the fact that Jerry was still so near would be even more disorientat-ing, she thought, remembering the chaos when she'd been twelve and the arrests had started for the first time.

She remembered her mother's reaction. Her tearing, aching sense of loyalty to someone who deserved none of it. Her distress that had spiralled downward.

Ouch. Don't go there, she told herself. Think of something else.

Do something.

She could just walk down to the refuge, she told herself. It wouldn't hurt. Five minutes. Just poke your nose in and make sure everything's OK, then get yourself back to minding your own business.

She'd expected the marine refuge to be peaceful. There'd been welfare officers and reporters with them all day, she knew. They'd be exhausted. They might even be in bed.

She entered—and was met by turmoil.

There was a little girl retching on the kitchenette floor. Marigold? She'd been discharged from hospital only hours ago, she thought, stunned. Darcy had released Marigold and David into their mothers' care.

A little boy was writhing and moaning on the couch by the window. Penny was bending over him. From the bedroom came the high, thin wail of another child in distress.

What on earth was happening?

Triage. Marigold was sobbing and retching and crumpling to the floor and she was four years old. That was where Ally went first.

She lifted the child to the sink, though by the look of the floor it was hardly worth it. Marigold retched until she could retch no more, then slumped backward into her arms.

'Mummy,' she whimpered.

Marigold was Lorraine's child. Ally looked around. Penny was still bending over…David? Yes, David. She was holding a bucket, and David needed it.

'Where's Lorraine?' Ally asked, and Penny gave her a despairing glance before turning back to her son.

'In the bedroom. She's ill, too. The kids have got stomach cramps and Lorraine's as bad.'

Ally looked down at David. He was ill but he was still strong enough to hold up his head.

He could be left to his mother.

Still cradling the whimpering Marigold, Ally walked through to the kids' bunk room.

Two of the kids were sitting up in bed, bemused, as if they were wondering what all the fuss was about. Another child was bent over another bucket, and Lorraine was clutching her stomach as if she'd like to join him.

'What the…?'

'It must be food poisoning.' Cornelia, the refuge caretaker, appeared at her shoulder with a suddenness that made her jump. 'One of the guys—Greg—has cramps as well. I've been trying to ring Dr Rochester but he's been out of town. He was just back in calling range when a local farmer rang to say he'd caught his hand in a post-driver, and Dr Rochester had to go out again.'

Ally sorted the urgent from the dross. Darcy wasn't coming. All the other information was superfluous. 'Are they sending someone from the hospital?'

'There's no one to send. Unless they call in emergency staff, and they'll only do that in an emergency.'

Oh, great. Define emergency.

Why should she define anything? Ally asked herself, savage at the way medical need was being thrust at her. She was a massage therapist. She wasn't a doctor. She should have ripped up her registration long ago.

No.

She was a doctor whether she liked it or not, she acknowledged. She knew what was life-threatening.

The child she was holding was ill already. Released from hospital today, a dose of food poisoning could dehydrate her to the point of death.

Define emergency? She had.

'What have they eaten?' she snapped.

Cornelia was a middle-aged woman who was slow at the best of times. She took her time to think. While she did, Ally stared around at the kids and at Lorraine.

The little boy was in distress, but he didn't look limp. He was wailing and his mother was trying to comfort him. She wasn't in a position to do much. Marigold made a feeble gesture that she wanted to go to her mother but Lorraine was clutching her stomach in a gesture that told Ally she was feeling as dreadful as her children.

'Mummy's not well either,' Ally told her, firming her hold. 'You must all have tummyaches. It's just as well I'm a doctor.'

What was she saying? Admitting that she was a doctor for the second time in two days?

Help. Her decisions as to her future were being eroded by the second. But Marigold needed reassurance more than anything.

'What did you guys eat today?' she asked, and Marigold managed to answer before Cornelia answered for her.

'Everything,' she whispered. 'We ate everything.'

'The baker put on a huge spread for your party,' Cornelia said, finally getting it together. 'There was so much food, and many of the locals contributed more. There was lots left, so they brought it here. We had sausage rolls, hot dogs, cream puffs, éclairs, lamingtons, sponge cakes...'

Marigold cringed and Ally took a deep breath. Sausage rolls. Hot dogs. Sure, they could hold bacteria. If they did then she could well be writhing on the floor in a few hours herself, but it was much more likely that bacteria had nothing to do with this.

She remembered the food Jerry had decreed they eat all those years ago. Why would he have changed? He wouldn't, she thought. He'd have access to all their pensions but any spare money would be his to do with as he wished.

Every single one of these people was seriously malnourished. That was why the chickenpox had hit so hard.

So they'd been starved for years—and then given a feast of hot dogs, cream puffs, éclairs. As much as they could eat.

Still holding Marigold, she knelt before Lorraine so she was right in her field of vision. The little boy could see her, too.

'Lorraine.'

Lorraine looked up, her face desperate. 'Someone's poisoned us,' she whimpered.

Great. Marigold jerked in her arms. The child might be only four years old but she knew what the word 'poison' meant.

Terror.

'No,' Ally said strongly. She might be wrong, but she doubted it, and even if she was… What these people needed most was reassurance. They'd been thrust out of their way of life, put at the mercy of the townspeople who Jerry would have taught them to fear.

'I'm a doctor,' she told Lorraine, in a voice that was stronger than the one she'd used with Marigold. 'It's my guess that you've been eating the same food for years. Rice and a tiny bit of free-range chicken and the vegetables you've grown yourselves. Nothing else. You've eaten the same thing day after day after day, and then today you've been given a feast. You've had pastry and sweets and butter and rich, fatty meat, and you've all eaten too much, too fast for your stomachs to handle.' She gestured to the children who weren't ill. 'It's a miracle that all of you aren't vomiting. I'll give you injections of Maxolon—that'll stop the vomiting—and I'll set up a drip for Marigold as I'm worried that she'll go back to being dehydrated. Maybe David needs a drip, too. But I'm afraid there's not much else I can do. Your bodies are just going to have to get rid of what they can't handle.'

Lorraine groaned. She clutched her stomach again and then she sat back and gazed up at Ally in disbelief.

'I ate six lamingtons,' she managed, and groaned again.

'Oh, dear.' Ally smiled, but Marigold's hands were clutching her around her neck and she felt her little body go rigid as once more she started to retch.

'Can you ring the hospital again?' she asked Cornelia. She was thinking through the options as she spoke. She could take Marigold to the hospital but all of them needed supervision. It would be easier if she settled them here. Also, it'd be much less traumatic than to try and transport people who were already so ill. 'I want a nurse down here,' she said. 'I want saline drips and Maxolon. Enough for half a dozen patients. Tell them what's happening.'

'They won't send a nurse,' Cornelia muttered, glancing out with disbelief to the state of a kitchen Ally suspected she was usually deeply proud of. Not now. 'I told you. They don't have spare staff.'

'They'll have people they can call on in an emergency,' Ally told her. 'This is an emergency.'

'But Dr Rochester—'

'Dr Rochester is out of town. He's not here and I am, so you'll just have to be content with Dr Westruther.'

Then she added a rider under her breath before she reached for the phone herself to make the call Cornelia was so reluctant to make.

'And you'll have to be content with Dr Westruther, whether Dr Westruther likes it or whether she doesn't.'

CHAPTER NINE

DARCY walked into the refuge and stopped dead.

Ally was scrubbing the kitchenette floor.

The sitting room was deserted. A fire still crackled in the grate, but the only other sign of life was Ally's backside. It was an unmistakable backside. Her trousers were stretched tight over what was really a very nice posterior. The sleeves of her windcheater were hauled up almost to her shoulders. Her blonde hair was escaping from the twist she'd had it in earlier in the day, and it was wisping forward.

She had a scrubbing brush and a bucket of steaming water, and she was scrubbing as if her life depended on it.

The place stank. That was the only sign that anything was wrong.

Darcy had brought Will Daly down to the hospital to be told there was drama at the refuge, but Will had lost too much blood to leave. He'd had to cross-match and set up a transfusion and it had been half an hour before he'd been able to find out for himself what was happening.

'Ally,' he said—tentatively—and she turned. When she saw who it was, she sat back on her heels and she glared.

It was some glare.

'I might have known,' she said with loathing. 'I have two square feet of kitchen floor-space left to scrub and, hooray, here comes the cavalry. The great Dr Rochester, arriving just when he's most needed. What a hero.'

'Steady on,' he said, trying not to smile. 'Are things OK?'

'Fine. No thanks to you.'

'I've been busy.'

'Doing something nice and clean?' she demanded with gentle mockery. 'A squashed finger, I hear. I bet someone else scrubbed the floor.'

'His wife,' he admitted.

'How is he?' she asked, sarcasm fading.

'Bad. But I'd say it's mostly repairable bone damage. Not nerve as far as I can tell. It's Will Daly. He says he knows you.'

'I went to school with Will.' She brushed her wispy hair behind her ears. 'He always beat me at marbles. So he'll be OK?'

'He has all major feeling. He'll need an orthopaedic surgeon.' He smiled. 'If he's lucky, his skill at marbles will hardly be impaired.'

'Good.' She managed a smile in return but she was looking distracted. 'You'll send him to Melbourne?'

'I've arranged for him to be taken to St Margaret's tomorrow. They have the best orthopaedic unit and Robert can go with him.'

'The guy with the face?'

'Mmm.' Darcy strolled over and looked down at her shining floor. 'Is he OK?'

'He didn't join in the feast,' Ally told him. 'The pain relief you've given him is so welcome that all he's done is sleep.'

Darcy's smile grew a trifle rueful. 'I guess we should be thankful for small mercies.' He gazed down at her for a moment. She looked almost unreal. Sitting on the floor with her scrubbing brush, looking like...

Looking like what? He didn't know.

Looking like Ally.

He gave himself a swift mental kick. Hell, where were his thoughts? Concentrate on medicine.

'Robert's not a priority public patient for transport,' he told her, struggling back to medical imperatives. Somehow. 'But his face is urgent and this will get him into the system fast. I couldn't get him on the chopper with Marilyn this morning, but he can go by road with Will tomorrow. I'll send Kevin as well. His throat's fine but he needs urgent psychiatric care. He and Robert can keep each other company.'

He gazed around at the tidy sitting room, and through to the bedrooms beyond. Only one bedroom was still lit, and there was a gentle murmur of a comforting voice coming from the dimly lit bedroom. Betty? 'Tell me what's happening here.'

'Will's safely in hospital?' she asked.

'Yes. I brought him in half an hour ago and they told me I was needed here. I came as fast as I could.'

'What, you? Needed?' She seemed to abandon interest in him as she turned back to her scrubbing. 'I can't imagine why.'

'Ally…'

'Betty's here,' she told him. 'As you can hear. She's watching Marigold. I've given Marigold Maxolon but she's still retching. I don't want her left alone. She's exhausted to the point where she's almost unconscious, and I don't want her choking.'

'You've set up a drip?' he asked cautiously, and she scrubbed a bit more before she answered.

'A drip. Yes. A drip. Three drips, Dr Rochester. Two very sick kids, another mildly ill and Lorraine. Robert didn't join in the feast and the others must have cast-iron stomachs. Tell me, was it your idea to send sick children home from hos-

pital and give them a welcome-home feast of chocolate éclairs and lamingtons?'

'Not a good idea, huh?'

'Not.'

'If it's any consolation, I didn't order the lamingtons.'

'It's not a consolation.' She gave her floor a
final swipe and then sat back and surveyed her
work. 'Finished. Darcy, haul that window wider.
It stinks in here.'

'You've only just noticed?'

Her glare returned. 'I haven't only just noticed,
as a matter of fact. And as well as this place stink-
ing, I stink as well. Marigold was sick all over me.'

'Why isn't Cornelia scrubbing?' he asked, and
got a look that said he was thick.

'The smell of vomit makes Cornelia retch,' she
told him. 'Which is a lot of use, I don't think. And
scrubbing floors isn't in Betty's job description unless it's in a hospital and it's imperative, and even
then she'd rather not. So she's caring for the sick.
Which leaves the massage therapist scrubbing.'

'Good old massage therapist.' He couldn't help
it. The corners of his mouth twitched all by themselves. 'Did they train you in scrubbology in massage school?'

'Where would you like this brush?' she asked,
and raised it.

He laughed and stretched out a hand to help pull her up. 'Hell, Ally, I'm sorry.' And then his nose wrinkled.

'Don't say it.' She heaved her bucket over to the sink. 'Well, that's it for me. Dr Rochester has arrived and I can go back to being a massage therapist.' She wiped her hands on her trousers and took a deep breath. 'Enough. I'm out of here. I've written up all medications on the chart I've left with Betty. Check what I've done. They're your patients and I shouldn't have interfered, but if you will hare round the country fixing broken fingers when you should be down here scrubbing floors…'

'I wasn't just fixing broken fingers.'

'No?' She turned back to him and raised her eyebrows. 'If you're about to tell me that you stopped for a while to admire the moon over the sea then I don't want to know.'

'I was organising accommodation.'

She stared at him. And then she seemed to come to a decision. 'This is nothing to do with me,' she told him. 'You need to check your patients. I need to slope off home and have a shower.'

'Do I need to check the patients immediately?'

'Unless you trust me.'

'I do trust you.'

She blinked. 'I…'

'Of course I trust you. You're a fine doctor.'

'I'm not a doctor.'

He let that one slide. It was obviously ridiculous and both of them knew it.

'I've been organising accommodation,' he told her, cutting her off before she could figure out what to say next. 'Long-term accommodation for everyone. Including accommodation for you and your mother.'

She blinked again, owlish in astonishment. 'Sorry?'

'You heard.'

'You've been arranging accommodation for me and my mother?'

'I assume that's what you want,' he told her, watching her face. 'A furnished house where you can have your mother with you?'

She was dumbfounded and it showed. 'What do you know about my mother?'

'A lot,' he told her, his voice gentling. He was treading on eggshells here and he was aware of it. It behoved him to be very, very careful. 'I talked to Sue today.'

'Sue?'

'Marilyn's daughter. She was very fond of you when you were kids.'

Ally's suspicious face softened. 'I... She was great. Sue and her mum and her dad. They were wonderful. That's why...'

'Why you outed yourself as a doctor to help Marilyn?'

'It might have been.' She hesitated, as if she was considering whether to talk or not. 'What did Sue say?'

'Not much. But enough. What she and Betty and you yourself told me made me make a few more enquiries.'

'You have no right.'

'No,' he said seriously. 'I don't have any right. But it's a hell of a story, Ally. Your mum had it so tough. Your grandfather washed his hands of her and abandoned her to Jerry. She couldn't break away herself but she gave you into your grandfather's keeping because she was afraid for your welfare. Her life must have been the pits.'

'She let me go,' Ally whispered. She turned away, ostensibly to lift the empty bucket from the sink but he knew in reality it was to give herself some space. Her voice was so low he could hardly hear it. 'As a child, I didn't realise what a sacrifice it must have been,' she whispered. 'The whole thing. Leaving my grandfather in the first place so I wasn't aborted, and then swallowing her pride and bringing me back.'

'She couldn't break away, though, could she?'

'Jerry was the only security she knew. My grandfather wouldn't exactly have killed the fatted lamb when she reappeared with me. His anger was vicious and it's a wonder he agreed to keep me at all.' She swallowed. 'And then…when I was small I was stupid enough to resent her. Stupid enough to hate her for sending me back to my grandfather. I even sided with my father.'

'Your father wanted you?'

'My father always wanted me to stay with them,' she told him, scrubbing at the sink with a dishcloth. 'It was only my mother who was afraid for me. I was sick when I was four—an infection that turned septic—and it frightened her. Apparently she threatened them. She said if they didn't let her leave me with my grandfather, she'd go to the police. She'd tell them everything she knew about Jerry. But she went back. And by the time my grandfather died, my mother was ill.'

'She's been diagnosed with almost crippling depressive illness,' he said gently—and waited.

At the sink, Ally was pleating the dishcloth with care. 'How did you find that out?'

'The locals knew your mother was institutionalised—that's why you were put into foster care when you were twelve. But now…'

'She hasn't been in an institution for six years,' she whispered. 'Not since I graduated as a doctor.'

'I know that.'

'How?' The dishcloth was being folded into smaller and smaller pleats.

'I have friends in the mental health services.' He shrugged. 'And in the police force. Sergeant Matheson obtained the case notes from Jerry's arrest when you were twelve, and we went from there. And I know. It's totally unprofessional, but when I made some tentative enquiries about your mother and added that I was worried about you, I got an earful. About how you'd taken her out of the institution the minute you started earning. You put everything into her care.'

'I tried to give her a life,' she whispered. 'She gave me one.'

'But—'

'But nothing,' she said, suddenly turning fierce. She turned on him then, her anger blazing. 'Fifteen. Fifteen! Seduced by a man who was twenty years older than her. Kicked out of home by her father, forced to live with that...with that...' Words failed her. She took a deep breath, fighting fury. 'And then she gave me up. She gave up her little girl. I remember, you know. I remember her bringing me here and Grandpa being cold as ice and her sobbing and saying he had to take care of me, it was his duty. She said it was Grandpa's duty to care for me but it was more than that. It was his duty to care for her.'

'But it's not your duty.'

'Don't give me that,' she flashed. 'Don't.'

He hesitated. He was pushing too hard, he decided. Change tack.

'Tell me about you and medicine,' he said, and waited.

There was a long silence. It stretched on and on. She wasn't going to answer him, he thought, but then…

'I decided it was the only way,' she told him. She was leaning against the bench, her hands clenching and reclenching at her sides. He felt an almost overwhelming urge to walk forward and take those clenching hands in his, but he didn't. There was a look on her face that told him she'd run a mile.

'From the time I was little, I was taught that medicine was the answer,' she said dully. 'My mother said Grandpa could look after me because he was a doctor. She couldn't look after me but Grandpa could. So I figured the way I could look after us was to be a doctor, too. Maybe I was naïve. But Grandpa… He kept saying Mum could have been a success. She could have been a doctor. It was like all our problems wouldn't exist if only she'd studied medicine. Stupid, isn't it? But it was something I held onto through the whole nightmare of childhood. When I was with Grandpa and I was miserable, I read his textbooks. When I went into foster care, I studied and studied. If I could just get to be a doctor, I thought, it'd solve all our problems. I could take care of my mother like no one ever had. I could take care of both of us.'

'But…it didn't work?'

'No,' she said flatly. 'Of course it didn't. It was a child's dream. It was my grandfather's horrid legacy and it backfired.'

'What went wrong?'

'Mum came to live with me,' she said drearily, as if it was old history that had long lost interest through retelling. 'Yeah, I was a hot-shot medical intern. I worked hard and I earned more than enough to keep us both and it was all supposed to be good. But I couldn't get close to her. She'd look at me like she was seeing something else. She sat in my gorgeous apartment, day after day, and she did nothing. She just sat. Like she was already dead. And then…'

She faltered, but somehow she forced herself to go on.

'I passed my obstetric exam,' she told him. 'By that time I was starting to treat her as part of the furniture. I was hardly trying to reach her any more. Anyway, the night of my exam results, I came home jubilant, bringing champagne and lobster and chocolates. The guy I was dating came with me. He was a neurosurgeon and I was an obstetrician. Two fantastic success stories. Still Mum just sat there. Just...looking. And that night...' Her voice hushed almost to a whisper. 'That night she attempted suicide.'

'Ally...' He made a move toward her but she flinched. As if she was afraid. He stilled. He mustn't push. He mustn't. This was far too important.

'She left a note.' Ally swallowed and stared down at her hands. 'She said that I had a life now, just like Grandpa's, and she was proud of me. But my life had nothing to do with her. Nothing had anything to do with her. I was a success and I didn't need her. I'd never needed her. She'd stuffed everything.'

'Hell, Ally.'

'I didn't know what to do,' she whispered. 'All the reasons I'd done medicine... Suddenly they didn't mean anything. She took an overdose of aspirin—hardly an inspired choice for a suicide. She went into kidney failure and for a week I thought I'd lost her. My boyfriend told me if she lived then I should walk away. Get her committed back to that awful place she'd been in. It would have been so easy. But I sat through that awful week and I thought of all the people who'd walked away from her in the past. And I couldn't.'

'Of course you couldn't,' he said gently, and she flashed a suspicious look at him as if she thought he was humouring a child. But she continued, her voice full of remembered pain.

'Anyway… One of the nurses in the birth unit I was working in was a trained massage therapist,' she told him. 'I used to watch her rubbing the babies and massaging the mothers who were traumatised by the births and couldn't sleep. Liselle did her massages in her own time, but she loved doing them and so did the mothers and babies. When I'd been sitting in Intensive Care for three days, waiting to see if Mum would live, Liselle came to see me. I was exhausted past reason. So she just sat there, and she rubbed my hands and my shoulders and I felt myself relax. It gave me a tiny time out, but I so needed it. It was like a window out of a nightmare. And then I went in and I gently massaged Mum's face and neck—and she opened her eyes and she smiled at me. It was the best moment.'

'But…' He was trying to understand. 'Your medicine…'

'My medicine wasn't as important as my mother,' she told him. 'I took myself out and bought a massage book and I sat with her and I tried to reach her through touch. All the pills she was taking were useless. Touch reached her when nothing else would.'

'Medicine—'

'Oh, medicine works,' she told him, with a flash of something that might almost be humour. 'I'm not saying you're not needed, Dr Rochester. There's not a lot of call for massage when you're treating squashed fingers or obstructed labour. But for me, for now, massage works. Over the last couple of years I've sold everything I could to keep us afloat, and I've been back to college, learning massage as a professional.' She smiled then, a faint half-smile that was suddenly almost embarrassed.

'This time it was different,' she told him. 'It was something I could talk to my mother about. I came home every night and we discussed what was happening. I practised on her. Do you know how good that felt? It was wonderful. And the miracle is that she started learning, too. Just a little. Slowly. I practised on her and she practised on me. And by the time I qualified as a full remedial therapist, she had a certificate as well. She's a relaxation masseuse. Qualified. It may not seem very much to you, but I can't tell you...' Her voice broke. 'I can't tell you...'

She didn't have to tell him anything. He gazed at her face, and he saw a mixed-up combination of happiness and uncertainty and hope. Hope for a future she was working desperately hard to embrace.

No. She didn't need to tell him anything, he thought. He already knew.

He was falling in love.

Wrong.

He'd fallen in love.

When had it happened? He didn't know. He only knew that it had.

After Rachel had died, he'd thought it could never happen again—and maybe it hadn't. Because what he was feeling for Ally was a far, far different thing than the emotions he'd felt for Rachel.

Different but the same?

Two wonderful women. Two wonderful loves.

One who'd died six long years ago, and one who was gloriously, wonderfully alive.

And this was Ally. Ally, who'd pitted herself against the world and who was still fighting. Who stood there looking bereft and defiant and filthy and workworn and exhausted—and the most beautiful thing he'd ever seen. The most beautiful woman in the world.

Ally.

What he really wanted to do was to walk forward and take her into his arms. Right now. The sensation was almost overpowering and he had to physically haul himself back. She wasn't ready. He knew she wasn't ready.

'How's your mother now?' he asked, carefully, as if he might break something infinitely precious.

'She's with friends. But she's happy. She's cut right back on her medication. She smiles. She's cooking a little. She's seeing massage clients.'

'My friend told me that she's changed unbelievably.'

'Your friend?'

'Harry Rubenstein at Lawry Hospital.'

Her eyes lit. 'You talked to Harry?'

'Harry's a friend from way back. I tracked your mum through the institution records and they said she'd been discharged into Harry's care.'

'Harry's been wonderful,' she told him. 'It was Harry who suggested we might come back here. My mother was happy here once, and Harry thought it might help her even more.'

'Did Harry advise you to give up medicine?' he asked incredulously, and she shook her head.

'Of course he didn't. But I figured it out for myself. Like someone slapping you over the face with a wet fish—finally you get the obvious. Sure, make my mother better by re-creating my grandfather. By flaunting what she could have been in her face. I don't think so.'

'You're never your grandfather.'

'I tried to be.' She sighed. 'Anyway, that's my story. It's why I'm here. My mother's being cared for by friends for the first few weeks while I get myself settled.'

'Until you can offer your mother stability again.'

'Harry told you that?' Her anger flashed out. 'He takes a lot on himself.'

'He's no longer your mother's treating psychiatrist,' Darcy said gently. 'But he cares about you both. Deeply. And I don't blame him.' He hesitated. 'Can we go somewhere to talk?'

'No.' She swallowed and he saw another flash of fear behind her eyes. What was she afraid of? Him? The thought was almost unbearable. 'These people need you to stay here,' she told him.

'I—'

'If you have something to say, say it now. Here.'

'I told you. I've found you somewhere to live. I've found everyone a place to live.'

Silence. The tap was dripping behind her—a steady plink, plink. It was starting to worry him.

Or maybe…it wasn't the tap that was worrying him. He didn't know how the hell to start. He didn't understand her fear.

He had to say what she needed to know.

'You knew that Jerry's father owned much of the land around here?' he said at last.

She nodded. Still distrustful.

'I've been asking questions of the locals this afternoon,' he told her. 'It seems the old man still owns property.'

'The land on the ridge.'

'More. There's a farm on the promontory before you get to the lighthouse. There's a manager on it and it's where the Hatfields used to stay when they came to town. It's run as a dairy farm—it could be really productive, but the word is that it was being kept for Jerry in case he ever wanted a respectable living.'

'Why didn't Jerry take his people there?' Ally asked, puzzled. 'Instead of up to the ridge.'

'Jerry's been hiding. He was even hiding from his father. The old man's so angry I suspect if he'd known what Jerry was doing he would have turned his son in to the police himself.'

'How do you know this?' She was holding herself rigid, Darcy thought. She still looked as if she was about to run.

'I talked to him,' Darcy told her. 'I went out and spoke to the manager who's about a hundred, and he phoned old man Hatfield who's about a hundred and ten.'

'But…why?'

'I want that farm for these people,' Darcy told her, and she gasped.

'You're kidding.' And then, as she thought about it: 'He'd never agree. All old man Hatfield cares about is profit.'

'He cares about his name. According to the police, he helped Jerry escape overseas and he's helped him relocate at other times. Now…'

'Now what?'

'Now he's deeply ashamed. The farm's neglected. The rates haven't been paid. My suggestion—with the backing of the local councillors—is that the farm be signed over to the joint ownership of the people of Jerry's community, on the understanding that they don't press any charges against him.'

She thought about that, and seemed to find it wanting. 'Are there any charges they can lay against Jerry? Other than the ones that are already outstanding?'

'Who knows?' Darcy said. 'We certainly implied there were.'

'We? Who's we?'

'Me and Sergeant Matheson.'

'What on earth is this all to do with you?' she demanded, and he smiled.

'I'm a family doctor, Ally. I look for cures. Ever since yesterday I've been worrying about these people, thinking that their long-term trauma is going to be intense. They've been living together for years. They have no support. Split into separate units, I suspect they'd go the way of your mother.' She winced and his voice gentled. 'You know that's right.'

'I...I guess.'

'Anyway...' He still wasn't sure how she was taking this but he had to continue. 'While the councillors were talking about this—'

'The councillors?'

'Our town council consists of six people,' he said. 'Sergeant Matheson, Fred, Elaine, Myrtle, Hilda and me. You know them all. They certainly know you. The sergeant says he's the only one who hasn't had a massage yet and he wants the situation rectified.'

Her look of confusion deepened. 'So what were they talking about? Besides massage.'

'The farm, of course. And then you.'

'Me?'

He wanted to hug her. She stood there looking like a waif, a bereft child, but...more. She was all woman, he thought. A complicated mix of baggage, a magnificent masseuse, a doctor, a loving daughter, a spitfire who'd go after Jerry with a gun if she had to. A beautiful, desirable woman.

Ally.

He had to stay focussed. For the moment he had to stay focussed on not loving Ally.

Impossible ask.

'Ally, there's a fisherman's cottage down on the harbour,' he told her. 'Two up, two down. It belonged to Elspeth Murdoch who died last year and left it to be used by the council as they see fit. If we ever get funding we might set it up as a tourist information centre, but meanwhile it's furnished, it's lovely and it's vacant. We thought of it when we were trying to figure out where we could relocate Jerry's lot, but of course it isn't big enough. But then we thought of you.'

'I can't afford to rent anything yet.'

'That's just it.' He smiled, trying desperately to ease the tension in her eyes. 'The council has decided it needs a caretaker. We're offering it to your mother and to you.'

She stared, unbelieving. 'Why?'

'You feel badly about your mother,' he told her, his eyes not leaving her face. 'This town feels badly about you. There's a lot of guilty consciences round here. There's people who are whipping themselves that they didn't guess it was Jerry Hatfield come back to the ridge. And there are people who believe they should have stood up to your grandfather all those years ago—and then to your father when he took you away from where you belong.'

'But—'

'Your mother will be welcomed home with all honour, Ally,' he told her. 'You know that.'

She looked dumbfounded.

'What…what should I do?' she asked, and she sounded so lost that he had to steel himself to stay still. But some things were impossible not to say.

'You could let me kiss you,' he told her.

And waited.

'Kiss…'

'I'm falling in love with you, Ally.'

Mistake. He watched her face slam closed, shuttered against something that hurt.

'No.'

'No?'

'I can't…' She took a deep breath and then slowly turned back to the sink and laid her dishcloth down. When she turned back to him her face was inscrutable. Blank as a clean slate.

'You can't buy another doctor for this town,' she told him. 'Not with your cottage. Not with you.'

He froze.

'I'm not trying to buy another doctor.'

'I'm not going back to medicine.'

'You can't help yourself,' he said gently, gesturing through to the dimly lit bedroom. 'Tonight…could you walk away?'

'I must.'

'Would your mother deny you the right to be a doctor?'

'My mother denies me nothing. She never has.'

'So she'd support—'

'I don't want to be a doctor,' she told him, anger surging. 'I'm a massage therapist. It works. I love it. I love making people feel good. I love helping.'

'You helped tonight.'

'And now you're here and I can leave.'

'You can't walk away from what you are,' he told her. 'And you can't walk away from me.'

Her breath drew in on an angry hiss. 'What's that supposed to mean?'

He hesitated but it had to be said. 'It seems crazy, I know. It seems way too sudden. But I just have to look at you—your beauty, your courage, your humour… Ally, I can't help myself. I've fallen head over heels in love with you.'

Her face closed. He'd known it would. It was way too soon.

'Well, I don't love you,' she snapped. 'Why the hell would I? Men. I've had three of them in my life. My father, my grandfather and Jerry. Why would I possibly want more?'

'You had a boyfriend when you passed your obstetric exam,' he said, and her face stilled.

'So I did. That was when I was trying to pretend I could be normal. I could put away the past and take control of the future. But it's not going to happen. I'm happy now, and if you think I'm ever going to put my future in the control of a man—'

'Ally, I don't want to control you.' Damn, why couldn't he hug her? Why couldn't he touch her? But her whole stance spoke of fear and he knew to move would be a disaster. 'I don't want to change you. If you want to be a massage therapist…'

'I do.'

'Then why would I ask you to be anything else? I love you just the way you are, Ally,' he said softly 'How can I not?'

'Right.' Her lips tightened. 'Fine. So what am I supposed to do here? Fall into your arms? Move into my grandfather's house and play the doctor's wife?'

'Hey, Ally.' He was startled almost into laughter. 'I don't think we're going straight to the blue-rinse, bridge-playing, lording-it-over-the-town-as-the-doctor's-wife scenario just yet.'

'Don't laugh at me.'

'I'm not laughing at you. I could never laugh at you.'

'Then why mock me?'

'I'm not mocking you.'

There was a cough from the bedroom next door. Another. And then the sound of retching.

'Marigold's being sick again,' Ally said, almost conversationally. 'You're needed.'

He glanced toward the bedroom but Betty was there and she was surely capable of dealing with a retching child. She hadn't called him.

How could he leave Ally now, with so much left unsaid?

'I need you,' he told her.

'You need a medical partner. I'm not it.'

'I need *you*.'

'Right.' Her voice was an angry jeer. 'You've known me for how long?'

'Long enough.'

'Leave it.' She stared at him for a moment—almost desperately—and he took a step toward her.

'Darcy, don't.'

He hesitated, but he couldn't let her go. Not like this. He had to make her see what he was feeling. That he was a human—not some controlling male figure out for what he could get.

Ally moved then, trying to brush past him. His hands reached for her and he touched her face.

Gently. With no force. If she wanted to ignore him, she could. She could keep going.

She could leave.

But she paused.

There was a moment's stillness.

'Don't turn me into an ogre, Ally,' he whispered. 'I love you. I love you and I'll do whatever I have to do. I'll wait for however long it takes.'

And then, before she could move, before she could react, he bent his head and he kissed her.

He kissed her gently. Lightly. It was a feather touch of lips against lips.

And it was unbelievable. Unbelievably sweet. Unbelievably wonderful.

He'd known she'd feel like this, he thought as he cupped her face in his hands and pulled her gently against him.

He loved her.

The knowledge was intensifying by the minute. The certainty. It was like some great triumphant shout.

Or it was some sweet insidious whisper, a warmth of loving that embraced his heart. That seeped from her lips to his and filled his heart with something he'd hardly known he'd been missing.

Warmth meeting warmth.

Need meeting need.

Dear heaven, he loved her. His mouth moved on hers and he felt her respond. Her lips gently parted and her hands moved up to touch his face.

Ally.

Here was his home, he thought with sudden absolute surety. Here was his peace.

Ally.

The kiss couldn't last. It couldn't. There was a medical imperative—a sick child—and they both knew it. Ally pulled back, but as she did so he saw her eyes looked dazed. Her fingers lifted to touch her lips where his had pressed, and she looked at him as if she'd never seen him before.

There was a long silence. Things were changing. There was a conversation here, unsaid but real for all that.

A man and a woman and a sudden intense knowledge that things could never be the same again.

His heart was hers and she knew it. But it terrified her. He could see the terror.

'I don't… I can't…' she managed, and it was almost unbearable not to haul her into his arms and kiss away the dread.

But there was a soft call from the bedroom. 'Dr Rochester?' Betty was calling, and he could hear her reluctance. Whether or not she'd guessed what was happening out here, she needed him.

The medical imperative. He had to go.

'Ally, you can,' he said softly. 'Trust me. You can. We both can.' And then with a last, long, reluctant look he turned away—and it was the hardest thing he'd ever done in his life.

Marigold was waiting. Medicine was waiting.

Before he'd reached the bedroom door she was gone.

She walked out into the night, and had slammed the door closed behind her.

She was gone.

CHAPTER TEN

SHE walked.

Ally walked and she walked and she walked.

What on earth was happening? she wondered. What had she done?

She'd let Darcy kiss her.

Why?

She had no intention of having a relationship with Darcy Rochester. The concept was ludicrous. Unbelievable.

He was wonderful.

Her fingers lifted to her lips. She could still feel him. She could taste him. No one had ever made her feel…

Like she'd found the missing part of her whole.

That was a really stupid sensation. It made no sense at all.

Her feet had taken her down to the harbour. Her foot where the splinter had been removed was aching, but she ignored it. She had to see.

Down at the jetty were three terraced houses, each with different shutter colours—yellow, bright crimson and sky blue. The windows overlooked the cluster of fishing boats tied up at the wharf.

Two of the houses had window boxes dripping geraniums. The middle one had window boxes but the geraniums looked dead. Elspeth's house.

It was perfect.

She couldn't do it.

She walked on, down onto the wharf. Most of the fishing fleet was out but a couple of older boats were still swinging lazily at their moorings. She climbed onto the deck of the one closest to the harbour mouth, then sat and hugged her knees and stared out into the night.

This was where she'd come as a child to take time out. To try and sort out her head.

This was where she'd made the decision that she had to be a doctor, she thought ruefully. This was where she'd decided she had to lead her grandfather's life.

Could she go back to that life? To medicine?

If she stayed close to Darcy—if she stayed here—then she'd be drawn back into it. How could she not? And where would that leave her mother?

Her mother was only fifteen years older than she was, and in these last few months Ally had discovered something stunning. Elizabeth could be a friend.

It had been an amazing revelation. As they'd learned massage together, they'd discovered each other. Her mother had a keen, dry sense of humour, long suppressed by people who'd never laughed. Her mother shared her love of music— music that for almost thirty years she'd never listened to.

They talked now. They laughed together. They shared their enjoyment of what they were doing.

Elizabeth was finally starting to live.

And then along came Darcy.

'If I let myself love him, what would happen to Mum?' she asked the night, and there were no answers.

Or maybe there were.

Her mother would be an outsider. Again. Her daughter and her son-in-law would be a busy medical partnership and once again Elizabeth would be an onlooker. She'd be caught in a town while her daughter loved the town's doctor.

Great.

'I should never have come back here,' she whispered. 'It was really dumb. I've worked too hard over the last two years to risk it all because my stupid hormones are telling me I'm in love with Darcy.

'So now what?

'So get out. Go back to the city.

'Yeah, but…

'Yeah, nothing. You know it's the sensible thing to do.

'You can't give up Darcy.

'You must.'

She rose and walked to the bow rail, then leaned over and stared into the black depths of the sea below.

'My mother gave up nearly thirty years of her life for me,' she told the blackness. 'There's no choice. Get out while you can. There's nothing else to do. Leaving it longer will just make it harder.'

She flinched. Her windcheater wasn't enough to keep her warm in the cool sea air, or maybe she would have been cold no matter what she'd been wearing. Feeling ill, she left the boat and made her way up the main street to her rooms.

Her upstairs light was on.

She stared. Surely she'd left it off.

Darcy?

No. His car wasn't there. And he surely wouldn't have let himself in. He couldn't. She'd locked the place. The small spurt of hope that somehow he'd come...somehow he'd dissuade her...somehow he'd provide a possible solution to an impossible dilemma died almost before it was born.

Her door was locked. She must have left the light on herself. She let herself in and walked up the stairs with dragging steps.

She swung open the door to her living room—and her mother was lying on the bed, reading massage manuals.

'Mum.'

Her mother looked up and smiled. It was a smile that had disappeared for thirty years and it still made Ally catch her breath when she saw it.

At forty-five, Elizabeth was an older version of Ally. They were almost exactly the same height as each other. Until two years ago Elizabeth had been painfully thin but she'd filled out now, and her figure was as lovely as Ally's. Her hair was cut short, blonde wisped with grey, but her green eyes were Ally's, as was her smile.

She was wearing jeans and sweatshirt that almost mirrored Ally's everyday uniform.

'Hi,' she said. 'Surprise?'

Ally caught her breath. 'Yeah.' She shook her head and managed a smile in return. 'I'm surprised. How did you get here?'

'I caught the bus.' Then, at Ally's increased look of astonishment, she explained some more. 'I read the papers this morning.'

'You read about Jerry's arrest.'

'I certainly did. They finally have him behind bars.'

Ally hesitated. Seventeen years ago, when Ally had gone to the police and had Jerry arrested, her mother had disintegrated.

'You don't mind?'

'Of course I don't mind.' Her mother was still smiling. 'You're doing what I should have done when you were four years old but I didn't have the courage. I still thought I loved your father.'

'But…'

'Yeah, I collapsed last time,' she said. 'I'd made such stupid decisions. I'd lost so much. I was a different person then. But not now, Ally.' She sighed, held out her hands for Ally to help pull her to her feet and then hugged her. 'It's only taken me thirty years to figure out that I can get over Jerry—that damage can be cured.'

'Mum?' Ally hugged her back, then pulled away to stare at her as if she didn't believe what she was hearing. 'How…how did you hear?'

'I told you. I read the papers. And then I was massaging Esther Hardy this morning and we talked about it. Esther heard an in-depth radio interview with a Sergeant Matheson. She knew everything.'

'Yeah?' Ally glanced at her mother with caution. She'd never heard her like this. Lit up. Excited. She moved across to the sink and filled the kettle. Buying herself some thinking time. 'So what did Esther say?'

'She said that Jerry had been arrested here, and there were children who were really ill. She said there are arrest warrants out for him from everywhere. And she also said there's a whole community of people here that he's been controlling. Apparently one of the kids almost died and there's been a death in the past.'

'So you decided to come.'

'Esther got me thinking,' she said, and she prepared coffee mugs. For Ally's normally apathetic mother, preparing mugs was a pretty astounding thing to happen all by itself. 'Did you know Esther was deaf for thirty years?'

Ally frowned. The apartment they'd had in Melbourne was one of eight and the neighbours were friendly. During the last two years as they'd practised their massage, almost every one of their neighbours had volunteered to be massage guineapigs. Esther, especially, loved their massages. But until now she'd been quiet and not forthcoming about herself at all.

'I didn't know she'd been deaf.'

'She has one of those new cochlear implants,' her mother said. 'She's had it in for the last three years and she said it's like her life just started again. When she was sixty she started to hear again. Can you believe that?'

Cochlear implants were amazing, Ally knew. But where was this going?

'Anyway, I thought,' Elizabeth told her, reaching over for the kettle which Ally had forgotten to switch on, 'that if Esther could be brave enough to start again at sixty, surely I could do the same at forty-five. You know what Esther does now? She teaches at the deaf school. She teaches sign language to parents of kids who are deaf. She makes bridges, Ally.'

'Um… That's great.'

'Yeah, but I thought it's what I could do,' her mother said, in a tone she'd have used if Ally was slightly stupid. Which maybe she was. 'All these people Jerry's hurt… Maybe I could talk to them. Maybe I could even teach them a bit of massage. Maybe I could help.' She gave Ally the beginnings of an excited smile. 'You and I have created ourselves a life. Maybe I could show them that it's possible for them to do it, too.'

Maybe it was possible.

Ally lay and stared at the ceiling. By her side her mother was deeply asleep, worn out by the day's excitement. And exertions.

'How did you get in?' Ally had asked her, and her mother had actually giggled.

'I can get into every single building in this town. Remember, this is where I grew up. I shinnied up the oak. Someone I know taught me to pick locks and I climbed in the window.'

'Mum!'

'I have all sorts of useful skills,' her mother said with mock primness. 'Now it's time for me to start using them.'

So her mother was here. Her mother was excited. Her mother was really, really pleased to be back in the town where she'd been born.

And in the morning…

In the morning her mother would meet Darcy.

Ally stared up into the darkness and tried to figure out what on earth was going to happen. She stared up into the darkness some more.

And she kept on staring.

And then the phone rang.

It was well after midnight. If she'd been alone maybe she wouldn't have answered it, but Elizabeth stirred and Ally grabbed the receiver before it woke her mother.

'Ally?'

'Darcy.'

'That's the one,' he said, and his voice was almost cheerful. 'I was hoping you'd guess. Doctors get patients calling at midnight, but massage therapists don't much, hey?'

'What are you doing, ringing me here?'

'Where else would I ring you?'

'Go away.'

'I'm not going to go away, Ally,' he told her, and his voice became all at once serious. 'I know I rushed you.'

'No.'

'Yeah, I did,' he said ruefully. 'Telling you I loved you. The thing is that I'd just figured it out for myself and I got all excited.'

'Well, get unexcited. It's not going to happen.'

'It already has happened. I love you. And the way you responded... Hell, Ally, you're feeling it, too.'

'I'm not feeling anything,' she snapped, and there was desperation in her voice. 'I can't.'

'You can.'

'My mother's here.'

There was a moment's silence. 'Elizabeth's here?'

'She caught the bus. She climbed up the oak tree and picked the lock of my window.'

He whistled. 'Well, well. Bully for Elizabeth.' He thought about it for a moment. 'So she's started saving herself, then. That'll take a load off your shoulders.'

'You don't know what you're talking about.'

'No.' He hesitated. 'Or maybe I do. You're so afraid of the past.'

'I'm not afraid of the past,' she managed. 'I'm afraid of the future.'

'Now, that's just silly,' he said reasonably. 'You don't even know what the future holds. Except… me?'

He broke off on a crazy note of pathos, appeal and laughter, and it was all she could do not to slam the phone down. She should slam the phone down.

Why didn't she slam the phone down?

'We'll leave,' she whispered.

'Why would you leave? You've only just got here.'

'My mother… How do you suppose she'd feel if I fell in love with the local doctor? If I moved into my grandfather's house, made toast on my grandfather's wood stove…'

'Patted my dogs. Rocked on your grandmother's chair. Maybe, if you wanted…maybe even had our children?'

Had our children.

The words made her lose what little breath she had left. She was so shocked she held the receiver away from her and stared at it as if she was holding a scorpion.

Why didn't she hang up?

But Darcy was still talking.

'Ally, are you sure this is all about your mother?'

'What?' She replaced the receiver at her ear and put her spare hand up to rake her hair, distracted beyond belief.

'Is it about you?' he was asking.

'I don't know what you mean.' But maybe she did. She could almost hear the smile in his voice and she knew that if he was near, he'd be laughing. And maybe reaching to touch her.

'I love you, Ally,' he said softly. 'I love you. But, unlike you, I know what love is.'

'I—'

'I loved Rachel,' he said, overriding her interruption, and his voice was urgent. 'I loved her, Ally. We were part of each other. And when she died, part of me died, too. It hurt like hell.'

'I'm sorry, but—'

'The thing is,' he said, almost apologetically, 'that all you're seeing is the hurt. The men in your life—your grandfather, your father and Jerry— they're a hell of a bunch. They've let you down over and over. The townspeople here didn't protect you. Your mother wasn't able to. So you've built yourself this cocoon. If you love, then you get hurt.'

'Oh, please,' she whispered, staring down at her sleeping mother. 'What's with the psychoanalysis?'

'I did it as a minor during med,' he said, suddenly cheerful. 'I knew it'd come in handy some day, and what do you know? It has.'

'I'm not your patient.'

'No,' he said, and his voice was serious again. 'You're my love. You're my Ally. You're a wonderful doctor and a wonderful massage therapist and a wonderful daughter and karate expert and gun-blazer and toast-maker and floor-scrubber. But most of all you're you. I love you, Ally. Whatever you are. Whatever you do. If anything happens to you, I'll hurt like hell. If you hurt then I hurt and I'm exposed, come what may. Because I've made that commitment.'

'You're crazy.'

'I'm not crazy,' he said, 'because I know what's on the other side of loving. Sure, love can hurt, so much you almost break apart. But without love I'm nothing. Ally, these last six years without Rachel have been lonely, but they would have been so much worse—so much emptier—if I'd never loved Rachel at all. Rachel's love is part of me. It's part of who I am and it's part of why I can love again. Her love for me was a gift, but because I've been hurt I'm not about to walk away from love again.

Love's the most precious thing. And now…
tonight…'

His voice softened. 'Well, that's all I rang to tell
you. That I'm sure I'm right. I've fallen in love
with you and you have that love whether you want
it or not. Come what may. For ever. Don't use
your mother as a shield, Ally. Let's work it out.
Let *us* work it out. Everyone. You, your mother,
me, the people of this town… You're not on your
own any more. You've come home to Tambrine
Creek. You've come *home*. This is your home,
Ally. Now and for ever.'

And before she could say a word—if she could
have thought of a word to say, which she
couldn't—the receiver went dead.

She was standing in the middle of the darkened
room by herself.

'It's not true,' she whispered. 'None of it's true.'

He loved her. The thought was insidious in its
sweetness. If she could just take that step forward…

She wasn't alone.

Darcy was right. She wasn't alone. Her mother
was asleep on the mattress on the floor. And outside, somewhere, was Darcy.

Darcy.

Her love?

CHAPTER ELEVEN

BY THE time she fell into an uneasy doze it must have been past three, and when she woke the clock said eight-thirty.

Her mother was cooking bacon. The smell was all around the little room and Ally stared up in astonishment. Then she stared at the clock. She yelped.

'Help!' What had happened to her alarm? 'I have clients booked at nine.'

'I know,' her mother said serenely. 'I looked at your appointment book. It's almost full.' She beamed down at her daughter. 'You've done really well.'

Ally blinked. This was so unlike her mother that she could hardly believe it.

'I'll cancel them,' she said, and Elizabeth shook her head.

'Why should you? You have half an hour. I've cooked breakfast. Eat, shower, massage. In that order. There's no problem.'

'But you—'

'I have things to do, too,' she said serenely. 'If you'll tell me where Jerry's people are…'

'I'll come with you.'

'Why should you come with me?' Elizabeth asked, as if such an action was ridiculous.

'I could introduce—'

'I'll introduce myself. Now, one egg or two?'

Eggs. She had eggs, thanks to Darcy. Ally's thoughts were wildly tangential and they swung now to Darcy. Darcy had brought far too much breakfast for one morning.

Darcy loved her?

'Um…one.'

'You know, if you intend to start work at a reasonable hour, maybe you shouldn't stay on the telephone at all hours,' Elizabeth said, and Ally stared. She'd heard?

'I'm asking no questions,' her mother said, and a tiny smile hovered around the corners of her mouth. 'Not a question at all. But that's why I turned off the alarm. You had to sleep some time. And…did you know, when I tried to wake you just now, you called me Darcy?'

Work started dead on nine.

This was why she'd come, Ally reminded herself as she welcomed her first client. Setting up as a massage therapist anywhere but here would have entailed a long wait while the locals came to trust her. Here there was curiosity and goodwill—and eagerness to beat neighbours in saying they'd been to have a massage with 'our Ally'.

Our Ally.

She couldn't be our Ally, she thought, and her tangential thoughts were becoming desperate. Not if it involved medicine. Medicine had propelled her mother to suicide. How could she go back and risk that again?

'Can you give my neck a bit of an extra rub?' Doris Kerr was her first client for the morning. She'd come in for her own massage and was practically purring on the table. 'Don't bother with my legs. Legs are good but, oh, my neck…'

'You've got real tension knots,' Ally told her, kneading gently through the layers of tight muscles. 'You said you damaged a disc?'

'I fell over my dog,' Doris told her. 'Ten years back. We didn't have a doctor here then and I was in such trouble. I lay in bed for a week before my husband finally took me to the city. Then they put me in the orthopaedic ward. I lay in traction for three weeks with all these people who'd had car crashes or diving injuries or skiing accidents. Everyone kept asking what I'd done and I'd fallen over the dog. My poodle! Talk about humiliating.'

'I've seen people in real trouble with damaged discs after they sneezed too hard,' Ally told her, and Doris sighed again and sank into the kneading process with pleasure.

'That's what Dr Rochester said. He's been so comforting. For a while I travelled up to Sydney to see a physiotherapist, but now...'

'There are many things physiotherapists can do that I can't,' Ally told her.

'Yes, dear, that's what Dr Rochester told me when I asked if I should come to you.'

'Did he?' Ally asked slowly, and she had to force herself not to interrupt the gentle rhythm of her kneading.

'But he still said I should come,' she told her. 'He said it'd do my neck good to get the muscles warmed and mobile. I do tend to get a stiff neck. If it hurts then I don't move it, and it makes it worse.'

'He said I could help?'

'Well, of course he did,' Doris told her, as if the suggestion that he wouldn't have was astonishing. 'I mean, you're two professionals, aren't you? If you can't support each other, who can?' She wiggled on the table and gave another sigh of pleasure. 'Oh, my dear, that feels so good. Now...Henry says your mother arrived on the bus last night. Is that right?'

'That's right.'

'Well, isn't that just perfect?' Doris gave another happy wiggle. 'And they're saying you can have Elspeth's wee house, and then...' She stilled as if wondering whether she dared say something and then decided to go ahead anyway. 'They're also saying Dr Rochester is sweet on you. Already. Now, wouldn't that be something? If you could all live happily ever after.'

More of the same.

Followed by more of the same and more of the same.

The locals knew everything.

Betty must have overheard their conversation back at the refuge last night, Ally decided, and Betty had talked. As the morning wore on, more of her clients disclosed more about what was happening until she was almost ready to scream.

And then the phone rang.

While she'd been massaging she'd turned her phone over to the answering-machine. Now it was almost one and she'd finished for the morning. She washed the oil from her hands, listened to her messages and was just about to turn the machine back on so she could find some lunch—and find her mother!—when it rang.

'Ally.'

It was Elizabeth, and with that first word Ally knew something was dreadfully wrong.

'Mum…'

'You need to go to the police station.' Her mother was almost incoherent, and without thinking Ally switched into doctor mode. How to get information from someone who was panicking.

'Three deep breaths,' she ordered. 'Now.'

'I—'

'Breathe. Calm yourself down and then talk to me.'

There was a tiny hesitation and Ally could hear the breaths being taken. 'Sorry.'

'What's happened?'

'It's Jerry.'

'Jerry?'

'Kevin stabbed him.'

Ally was already shoving her feet into her outside shoes and was reaching for her keys with her spare hand. Now she paused, shocked into stillness. 'But Kevin's in hospital. Jerry's in jail.'

'That's just it,' he mother wailed. 'We're at the refuge. Dr Rochester was here. Ally, he's so nice. But someone just ran in from the police station next door. The policeman's wife. She's still here. She's so upset. She rang the hospital and they said the doctor was here and she just ran.'

This wasn't making sense.

'Is Jerry dead?' Ally demanded, and it was a learned shock tactic that worked.

'I don't know,' her mother whispered.

'So what's happened?'

'Kevin's supposed to be going by ambulance to Melbourne this afternoon.'

'I know that.'

'Yeah.' Her mother choked and Ally could hear the sound of a woman sobbing in the background. 'I… Anyway, while Dr Rochester was here looking after the kids, Kevin apparently headed over to the jail and said he desperately wanted to say goodbye to Jerry. The sergeant was out, but his wife let him into the cells. Just…to stand on the other side of the bars, she said. But as soon as Kevin got close he produced a knife and he started stabbing. Ally, the policeman's wife says Jerry's bleeding to death. Dr Rochester's gone to help, but by the sound of it he's got more than one stab wound. You have to go, too. You have to do something.'

But… This was Jerry! And her mother was weeping.

'You still care,' Ally breathed, appalled beyond belief. 'After all this time.'

The hiccuping sobs stopped. Immediately. There was a harsh gasp and then a change of tone that was unbelievable.

'What do you mean, I still care?' Her mother was suddenly yelling. 'Sure I care. I care that he goes to court and he gets convicted of every single crime he ever committed. Don't you dare let him die, Ally.'

'I'm not a doctor.'

'Of course you're a doctor,' her mother yelled. 'You're the best doctor I know. Now stop wasting time and get down to the police station and save that low-life's life. Now!'

It was only a block and a half and her ancient panel van took valuable moments to start. She ran and she reached the station in minutes.

Nothing. No cars. The door was wide open as if everyone had left in a hurry.

They must be at the hospital. She nearly didn't go in but there was a sudden harsh expletive from the back.

She went in—and the sight that met her made her flinch.

The cell door was wide open. There was a bunch of keys lying on the floor in a pool of blood.

Darcy was in the cell. He was bent over a crumpled form—Jerry—but he was glancing back over his shoulder. Talking. 'He's dead, Kevin,' he was saying. 'Leave it, mate. He's dead.'

Stop, she told herself. Take in the whole scene.

Kevin was crumpling back into the corner of the outer office. He was whimpering and his knees were drawn up to his chin. Still in his hospital pyjamas, he was blood-spattered and desperate.

He looked up at her now as if she was a spectre.

'I had to do it,' he whispered. 'I had to.'

He was holding a long, thin knife.

Was she first on the scene apart from Darcy? How fast had her mother called her?

Triage.

Ally glanced across at Darcy. Darcy looked up at her, and then at Kevin. His hands were pushing down hard on Jerry's chest.

He's dead, he'd said. But he was applying pressure.

The knife.

Darcy didn't move. At a guess, he couldn't. By the amount of blood, a major blood vessel was ruptured.

Was Jerry dead? Ally didn't think so. Her eyes moved again to the knife.

She walked across and knelt before Kevin.

'You've killed him,' she said softly, and she was carefully blocking his view of Jerry and Darcy. If Jerry moaned…

'I… Yes,' he whispered. 'He's dead. He says he's dead.'

'Then it's over,' she said. Still gently. Still feather-soft. 'It's over, Kevin. All the awful things that have happened are finished. You don't have to do anything any more.'

'But—'

'We'll look after you now,' she said. She put a hand on Kevin's bloodstained arm. 'You know it was me who had Jerry arrested. Let me take over now. Give me the knife, Kevin.'

He looked up at her with eyes that were blank with incomprehension—but then, like an obedient child, he held out the knife.

Dear God.

It was a vicious weapon. Some sort of filleting knife? He must have found it in the hospital kitchen, Ally thought. The knife had a long, vicious blade, with blood still thick along its length. It was pointed straight at Ally.

She swallowed—and then reached behind its point to take it by the handle.

He let it go.

Still she didn't move. If she moved, he'd be able to see Jerry, and if Jerry moved...

There was no sound from Darcy. She could hear him moving—he'd be frantically trying to stop blood flow—but he'd guess what she was doing.

He wouldn't mess it up by talking.

And then, blessedly, there was the sound of a car screeching into the main street, siren blaring. A skid of brakes.

Ally's eyes held Kevin's. She was ready to back away with the knife—to run—but she had a better chance of holding him with her eyes.

'We'll take care of you,' she told Kevin. 'Trust me. Jerry can't hurt you any more.'

A car door slammed. Feet against gravel, moving fast. A man's gruff voice, calling out. Sergeant Matheson.

She rose on feet that were decidedly wobbly, with the knife behind her back. She didn't take her eyes off Kevin.

'We're through here.'

'Kevin's killed Jerry,' she told the sergeant as he stopped in the doorway, appalled. She kept her voice carefully neutral, and behind her back and out of Kevin's view she held out the knife toward him. 'I think Kevin needs to go back to hospital now. Can you take him, Sergeant?'

He was good. His eyes swept the room, taking in the scene before him, but even before he was done he had the knife from her and it was pushed into a recess behind the desk. Then he went to kneel before Kevin.

'Help the doc,' he told her, glancing over to where Darcy was pushing desperately downward. 'I have this.'

It took the next three hours and all their combined skill to save the man Ally hated most in the world.

Kevin's first stab wound had been to Jerry's chest. Instead of backing away from the bars, he'd slumped against them, and Kevin had stabbed wildly at everything else he could. Luckily Jerry had fallen with his head out of reach, but his legs were a mass of deep lacerations, any one of which could have been fatal.

They almost lost him. Darcy had shoved a chair under his legs to raise them above the level of his heart, trying to stop the pressure of the blood surging out onto the floor.

For those first few minutes Ally worked with him. They put pressure pads on every spot they could find, fighting desperately to stop the bleeding.

It seemed an age, though in truth it was only three or four minutes, before back-up arrived, in the shape of Betty, driving her own car but carrying bags of saline and more dressings than Darcy's meagre doctor's bag provided.

The three of them worked on.

Sergeant Matheson took Kevin away but they didn't notice. Did Kevin realise that Jerry wasn't dead? Ally wondered, but it didn't matter.

He could still die. His blood pressure was dropping and dropping.

But somehow, somehow he lived on. To lose this much blood and live was almost miraculous.

Still they worked.

Finally Darcy sat back. The last of the spurting sources of blood had been quelled. Maybe there was a hope. The fluids were pouring in now, the IV line set to maximum. He had a chance.

Or did he?

'His trachea has moved,' Darcy said. He'd hardly looked at Ally. There'd been no time. The three of them had worked as a solid medical team, as if they'd trained together for years and were working in the emergency ward of some huge city hospital instead of in a lake of blood on the floor of the number one cell of Tambrine Creek police station. Now, though, Darcy had time to sit back and assess the whole situation.

His trachea had moved?

Ally finished taping a pressure bandage to Jerry's groin and looked up at Jerry's throat. The man was seriously overweight, his neck was pudgy but she put her fingers down and felt, and she could feel what Darcy meant.

Jerry's trachea felt as if it had shifted slightly to the left.

'His lung.' Darcy grabbed a stethoscope from the pile of equipment Betty had brought, and his face tightened as he listened.

'Tension pneumothorax?' Ally asked, and he nodded.

'It has to be. That first wound was to the lung. I could hear the pneumothorax before but didn't realise... The air's going straight out into the chest wall.'

Dear God. They all knew what that meant. A punctured lung causing a pneumothorax was serious, but a tension pneumothorax was far, far worse. The air that Jerry was managing to get into his injured lungs wasn't being exhaled. Neither was it escaping through the track of the wound. Part of it was escaping into the chest wall.

The pressure was building, shifting the trachea. Soon it would compress the heart and the other lung, causing it to collapse. And then...

Then death.

The ambulance officers were there then—two volunteer officers who were standing back in dismay, waiting to see whether they'd be transporting a corpse or a patient.

'Let's get him to hospital,' Darcy said grimly. 'I need to get a tube in there.'

'Can you?' Ally practically gaped. Inserting a cannula into a chest wall was a job for a surgeon, and a good one at that.

'I don't see that I have a choice,' Darcy said grimly. 'I've seen it done. Once. What do they say? See one, do one, teach one. Teaching's for tomorrow. For now... Are you assisting—*Dr Westruther*?'

There was only one answer to that.

'If you're going to be a hero, you need a heroine,' she said, and flashed an uncertain smile at Betty. 'How about you? You want to be a damned-fool heroine, too?'

'Who, me? I'm just here 'cos I like blood.' Betty grinned, and the awful tension dissipated for the moment. 'And I love watching heroes and heroines. My very favourite thing.'

The surgery Darcy performed was the stuff of nightmares. Injecting lignocaine. Using a cannula with trochar, inserting it carefully, painstakingly carefully through the chest wall. Hearing the rush of air. Connecting the cannula to an underwater seal and watching the water bubble. Knowing the air couldn't flow back up the tube.

Described like that, it almost sounded easy, Ally thought, but it was the finest piece of surgery she'd ever seen performed by a non-surgeon. That it had been done by a family doctor who'd last seen the procedure five years ago was unbelievable.

She couldn't believe Darcy had succeeded, and years later when he recalled doing it Darcy still shook his head in disbelief himself.

They didn't stop there. The slashes were deep and serious and no amount of pressure would stop some of them from seeping. Some of the slashes were down to the bone. The suturing took hours, and some would require further work from a plastic surgeon. Maybe he'd even need vascular surgery if he wasn't to lose a hand. But they managed to establish a blood supply of sorts, and when Darcy finally dressed the hand Jerry's fingers were encouragingly warm.

Finally they'd done all they could—and he was still alive. Ally could stand back from the table, push away her mask and think that maybe he had a chance of long-term survival.

'The helicopter's coming in now,' Betty told them in a voice that was far from steady. 'Medical evacuation's been arranged.'

'They'll have to fly low,' Darcy told her. 'The air pressure…'

'Do you want him to stay, then?' Betty was a fine nurse. She'd reacted with composure through everything. 'I didn't even ask—I just had Joe get them to come.'

'He needs to go,' Darcy said. He looked down at Jerry for a long minute. 'The lung needs an expert. The blood supply to the hand is none too stable. And the wound in his groin…he may well need a vascular surgeon to repair the damage if he's not to lose feeling. Let's get him out of here now.' He hesitated. 'What's happening to Kevin?'

'Ally told one of the nurses to give Kevin five milligrams of diazepam IV,' Betty told him, and he threw Ally a curious look.

'That's a lot of diazepam for a massage therapist to prescribe,' Darcy said with a wry grin.

'You're just lucky the massage therapist didn't take the whole lot herself,' Ally retorted. 'Though if there's any going now, I wouldn't mind at all.'

Finally, while Darcy assisted in loading Jerry into the ambulance for transfer to the helicopter pad, Ally went outside and spent five minutes just deep breathing. Nothing more. She couldn't believe what had happened.

She'd helped save Jerry's life.

Her mother had ordered her to do it.

Elizabeth.

She had to find her. All she wanted was to find herself a bolt hole and try and come to terms with what had happened, but the thought of what her mother must be going through steadied her. A bit.

Reluctantly she cleaned herself up as best she could and went to find her.

But Elizabeth wasn't at the refuge. Ally had to field a thousand questions before she could get away, but no one knew where Elizabeth had gone. She wasn't back at the massage rooms. By the time Ally got there, her stained clothes were starting to disgust her. She showered and changed. That made her feel normal—almost.

She kept on searching.

Where?

Where would she go herself?

Acting on instinct now, she walked down through the harbour. And there in her favourite spot in the whole world— on the bow of the oldest boat in the fleet—was Elizabeth.

Just sitting, hugging her knees as her daughter had done a thousand times before.

'I thought I might find you here,' Ally said, and her mother turned and smiled as if she'd been expecting her.

'You've been a while. Is he still alive?'

'He may well live.' Ally stepped across onto the boat and sat down beside her. They hugged their individual legs and stared out to sea.

'And Kevin?' her mother asked, watching the sea.

'He's tranquillised to the eyeballs. The police helicopter will take him to Melbourne. He needs a far better psychiatrist than we can provide here.'

'Poor Kevin,' Elizabeth whispered. And then she added a rider. 'He should have had a daughter.'

There was absolute silence at that. Ally could find nothing to say.

Finally she worked up courage, though. The question had to be asked.

'Why did you ask me to save him?'

'I thought I said. He has to go to trial.'

'But to ask me to be a doctor again...' She hesitated. 'I thought you loathed my medicine.'

Elizabeth turned and gazed at her in astonishment. 'Why would I loathe your medicine?'

'You tried to suicide. When I passed my specialist exam you tried to kill yourself.'

'That had nothing to do with your medicine.'

'Didn't it?'

There was another long pause. Elizabeth stared some more at the harbour mouth. There were swallows, swooping down in the failing light, doing aerobic feats among the mooring ropes as they searched for the twilight insects. The night was still and warm. Indian summer.

It couldn't last, Ally thought, and she hugged her knees tighter. Soon it would be winter. Soon...soon what?

Still she waited. She didn't push her mother. She'd learned a long time ago that Elizabeth kept her own counsel. She said what she wanted to say and nothing else.

'It was the touch,' Elizabeth whispered at last, and Ally tried to think about it.

'The touch?'

'Did you know,' Elizabeth said softly, 'that after my mother died no one touched me? She died when I was six years old. My father never hugged me. He never so much as held my hand. I was fifteen when I met your father. He told me I was beautiful. He hugged me. Of course I fell into his arms.'

'Oh, Mum.'

'Then at the commune there was nothing. No affection at all. Touch was sexual and there was nothing else. I lived in a vacuum for years.'

'Mum—'

'Then, when you had Jerry arrested, I fell apart,' she whispered. 'You were twelve years old and you stood up to him. You stood there that day looking like a little avenging angel, and I'd let you go. You were my daughter and I hadn't fought for you. I'd given you to my father and I knew you'd never been hugged either. I just folded. I'd failed. Nothing seemed to matter. It was crazy, but for me the next few years didn't exist. Even when you came to find me—when you took me to live with you—I wasn't aware.'

'You seemed dead,' Ally said gently, and her mother nodded.

'I think I was. But maybe we both were.' At Ally's look of confusion she tried to make herself clear. 'The night you passed that exam and brought your boyfriend back, you were so pleased, but we all just sat there. We drank champagne and we ate wonderful, expensive food and the guy you were with—I can't even remember his name—raised your gorgeous crystal champagne flute and said ''Congratulations'', but he didn't touch you. Not once. He hardly smiled. It was all so formal. I went to bed and I thought it didn't matter whether you were sleeping with him or not—you weren't touching him. And I thought, that's what I'd done to you. It was my dreadful legacy to my daughter.'

Ally could bear it no longer. She reached out and hugged. Hard. And Elizabeth hugged back.

'You see, this is the difference,' Elizabeth whispered. 'After the suicide attempt, I lay in hospital and you came in and you brushed my hair. You touched my face. I woke and you were rubbing my hands. Stroking. It was like a light had gone on. You were touching me. And I could touch back.' Elizabeth was still whispering but there was wonder in her voice now. 'I could hug you like I'm doing now. All at once I wasn't dead any more. Do you see what that meant?'

'I guess I do,' Ally said, a trifle unsteadily.

'You've changed, too,' Elizabeth told her. 'Jerry hurt us but he didn't destroy us. He took a huge chunk out of our lives but we're moving on.'

'Yeah.'

'You with your nice young man.'

That shook Ally out of her misty emotional haze. 'He's not my young man.'

'The whole town says he's nutty on you.'

'The whole town?'

'I've been talking to everyone,' Elizabeth said, and there was wonder as well as pleasure in her voice. 'All morning. You massaged and I talked. Welcome home, they all said. Welcome home. Doris Kerr came to find me after you finished massaging her this morning, and she took me down to the little house by the harbour.' She glanced behind her to the cute little house with the sad window boxes. 'I can't wait,' she said, and there was no disguising the eagerness in her voice. 'I can't wait to move in. The way I figure it, I'll spend a lot of time with Jerry's people, but that's where I'll live.'

'Where we'll both live,' Ally told her, but it was her mother's turn to look confused.

'I'd imagine you'll be living in Darcy's house.'

Ally drew in her breath. 'You mean Grandpa's house. Our house. Mum, how could I possibly do that? It has such memories.'

And it seemed that she was right. But memories meant different things to different people. 'My mother loved that house.' Elizabeth smiled and linked her hand with her daughter's. 'I made the best toast in that house.'

'Darcy still does.'

'Well, there you go, then.' Her mother smiled some more, her smile one of pure and absolute contentment. 'And speak of the devil...' She rose and waved and Ally turned to find Darcy standing on the jetty. He'd changed his clothes as well. He was wearing casual trousers and a big fisherman's sweater. Jekyll and Hyde were at his heels, the spaniels gazing up at him with adoration. And why not? He looked big and strong and capable.

He looked wonderful. Totally adorable.

He looked like Darcy.

'I'm guessing you two have things to sort out,' her mother told her. 'As do I.'

'Like what?' Ally was totally flummoxed.

'Well, for a start, if you think I'm sharing that mattress on your very uncomfortable floor for a single night more, you have another think coming,' Elizabeth told her. 'Doris has promised to help me set my new house up and we think I have time to settle in there this very night.'

'By yourself?' To say Ally was hornswoggled was an understatement.

'I'm borrowing Darcy's dogs,' Elizabeth told her, and actually chuckled at Ally's look of astonishment. 'I have it all arranged. Darcy thought I needed company and we thought that, seeing you and he...'

'Darcy thought...'

'OK.' Elizabeth held up her hands as if in surrender, but she chuckled again. 'I know. It's none of my business. But here are my friends.' Darcy reached out a hand to steady her as she climbed from the boat to the wharf, and she smiled up at him. Her smile was one of pure joy.

'Thank you for saving Jerry for me,' she said. 'None of us wanted his death on our consciences. So thank you for saving him.'

And then she turned and looked at Ally. Her smile deepened, and it was a look of pure love.

'And now...' she whispered, and she gave Darcy a slight push toward the boat. 'Now you go and save my daughter. She's just sitting there, waiting to be saved. So what are you waiting for?'

CHAPTER TWELVE

THEY were left alone.

Elizabeth took the dogs with her. She had their leads in her hands and they were bouncing along by her side as if they belonged there. Ally stared after them as if she couldn't believe her eyes.

'What have you done to my mother?' she whispered at last, and Darcy, who'd been standing on the wharf watching her watching her mother, grinned and swung himself down onto the deck.

'Nothing,' he told her. 'Not a single drug. Not a prescription in sight. You did the curing.'

'I think saving Jerry did the curing,' she managed, still watching her mother's retreat along the wharf. 'If he'd died…'

'I think your mother would be strong enough to cope with even that now,' Darcy said thoughtfully. 'She's an amazing lady. Mind, she didn't help very much in the initial drama. Talk about getting her priorities wrong. She called in the medics to a murder scene and didn't worry about calling the police.'

Ally frowned. 'Um…yeah.' The events of the afternoon had been puzzling her. 'I don't understand how I was second on the scene.'

'Third,' he told her. 'Helga Matheson, the sergeant's wife, was first.'

'So?'

'Helga let Kevin in to say goodbye to Jerry. Kevin produced the knife and stabbed him. So she went screaming next door for help, and next door was the refuge. But instead of saying there was a man still wielding a knife and he was still stabbing, she said that Kevin had stabbed Jerry, he was bleeding to death and I had to go. Everyone at the refuge—me included—assumed the sergeant was on the scene and he'd sent his wife to fetch me. So I went alone. If your mother hadn't decided you'd be needed, and if you hadn't agreed to come to help—and come fast—heaven knows what might have happened.'

'If Kevin had realised Jerry was still alive, he might have attacked again,' Ally whispered.

'Yeah. I didn't see the knife when I walked in. He was standing back from the bars looking appalled. I grabbed the cell keys from the desk and let myself into the cell. He made no move to stop me. Jerry was spurting blood and I had to move fast.'

'So you helped Jerry first.'

'Yeah.' He gave a wry grin. 'But I wasn't noble. I was just stupid. As I said, I didn't see the knife and I wasn't thinking. I hadn't realised Kevin would think he was dead. After all, any medic would know that with the sort of blood flow I was facing the heart had to be pumping.'

He hesitated and he was suddenly taking her hands in his and holding them as if he urgently needed to reassure himself that she was here. She was real. She was alive. 'And then you came,' he said softly. 'My Ally. You came and you saw the threat and you disarmed a potential murderer.' He leaned forward and kissed her lightly on the lips. It was a feather kiss, but it was so important. It warmed parts of her that she hadn't realised were cold. 'Well done, you,' he whispered. 'My Ally.'

'I didn't—'

'You did,' he said, and he kissed her again. 'We're a partnership, Ally.'

'So my mother says,' she managed. Just. How was she supposed to make her voice work? she wondered desperately. How was she supposed to make anything work? It wasn't possible. Not when Darcy was looking at her like that. Not when he was kissing her as if he loved her.

As if he truly believed that they belonged together.

It was an amazing thought. It was a concept that was so overwhelming it was almost frightening.

'You're angry?' He raised his brows and he smiled at her in that heart-flipping way he had that made her heart do backward somersaults, one after another. Try as she would to make it behave itself, it kept right on somersaulting.

'My mother is organising my life,' she managed with what she hoped was asperity. 'And you...' She fought for something she could be angry about. 'Lending your dogs to my mother without so much as a by your leave.'

'It seems your mother's gone and cut the apron strings,' he said, smiling at her with gentle humour. 'Your mother...taking my dogs for a walk without asking your permission first. Tch, tch.'

'Don't laugh at me.'

'I'd never laugh at you.' His smile died. His hold on her hands tightened, and the look in his eyes made her somersaulting heart stop its somersaulting and almost stop beating. 'How can I laugh at you?' he asked. 'I'll laugh with you, my Ally. Now and for ever. I'll laugh with you and I'll live with you and I'll share my life with you. With all honour. I love you.'

Her heart not only had stopped beating, it had stopped existing. This wasn't real. It couldn't be real. That this man could say those things. 'But—'

'You know, there's always buts,' he said, almost conversationally. 'You've been telling me you want to live here but you can't be a doctor. You can't be a doctor's wife. Well, I've decided the buts are OK. You don't have to be a doctor. You don't have to be a doctor's wife. You can just stay as Ally. Then it's up to me. You don't have to be a doctor's wife but…can I be a massage therapist's husband?'

She gasped at that, but suddenly, as if from nowhere, came belief. This was real. He was sitting on the deck of her favourite old boat, and he loved her.

Darcy Rochester loved her, no strings attached.

Her crazy heart started up again somehow, but this time it was doing handsprings.

'You're kidding.'

'Nope.' He was still smiling at her, with that wonderful smile that was a caress all on its own. 'I've been doing my homework,' he said, and there was a sudden mock smugness in his tone. 'I reckon I can start being your helpmeet straightaway. I know my herbs. What would you like as I give you your massage, my sweet? Angelica for gout and flatulence? Or cypress for constant running of the nose?'

She choked. 'You're crazy.'

'No.' He tugged her against him so her breast curved against his chest. She could feel the strength of him—the sheer arrant maleness. 'No, I'm not crazy. I'm in love. I'm in love with you and I believe—and I really, really hope I'm right here, Ally, because if I'm not I'm in all sorts of trouble and I don't know where to start—that you love me right back. Please.'

Silence. He was holding her, waiting for her response. Just holding her. Touch, she thought suddenly. It was the most important thing.

Darcy's touch.

His love.

'I looked up from Jerry this afternoon,' he said softly, and his voice was suddenly unsteady. 'I'd run in and gone straight to him and I hadn't checked. I saw Kevin but Jerry was bleeding to death in front of my eyes and he had to be the priority. That took over. When you walked in, all I felt was relief. And then I looked up and saw that damned knife. Hell, Ally... When you moved your body between Kevin and me, I swear it was all I could do not to launch myself across the room. I knew it was mad. I knew our best chance lay in having him believe Jerry was dead and I had to stay where I was. But, dear heaven, Ally, you were within reach of the knife. You were between him and his victim and I never want to be that terrified again.'

She couldn't bear that. She couldn't bear the pain in his eyes.

'You've lost once,' she said softly, reaching up to take his face in her hands. To take away that look of remembered horror. 'To risk that again… Darcy, how can you possibly love me?'

'How can I not?'

She looked at him for a very long moment but it was her turn now. Her turn.

She took his face strongly between her hands, she stood on tiptoe—and she kissed him.

She kissed him with all the love in her heart— and the beginning of the rest of her life started right then.

It wasn't very often that a mother got to be a bridesmaid at her daughter's wedding.

'But I feel like you're my friend and I don't feel ready to be the mother of the bride,' Elizabeth had declared, so at this most wonderful of weddings they compromised. She gave Ally away but she also stayed by her side as her attendant. Mother and best friend rolled into one.

The wedding took place in the little stone church in Tambrine Creek's main street. This church had seen generations of their family wed, baptised and buried.

It was right that Ally should be wed here. More, it was perfect. It was almost winter, but on this day the sun came out to shine on them all.

How could it not come out? The whole town came out. Everyone was invited and everyone was in a mood to sigh in pleasure.

And there was almost as much attention paid to Elizabeth as there was to her daughter.

As mother of the bride cum chief attendant, Elizabeth's dress was beautiful—pale apricot shantung, a dress the like of which Elizabeth had never worn in her life. It was a fairy-tale dress and she and Ally had taken as much care to choose it as they had the glorious dress of white shot silk that Ally wore.

Elizabeth looked beautiful and radiantly happy.

Ally looked stunning.

They almost looked like twins.

Well, why not? Elizabeth was blooming with newfound confidence. Already her little massage business was booming. She had more clients than she could handle.

Robert was one of her favourites.

Robert's face was healing now after extensive skin grafts. He'd returned to Tambrine Creek to move to the farm which the rest of Jerry's people were already turning into a successful commercial venture. Elizabeth walked out to see them most nights—but it hadn't taken many nights before Robert had started walking her home.

It'd take time, though, Ally thought as she watched their relationship grow. They'd been under a shadow for so long that neither was brave enough to trust. But Robert had taken to his role as farmer with skill and commitment. It was only a matter of time before he took on a share farm of his own, and then the future would be his to share with whoever he pleased.

He was waiting now, in one of the front pews. Ally knew that as she walked down the aisle Robert's eyes would be on Elizabeth. Not on her.

Which was how it should be. She was truly content.

Ally's attendants were fussing now—all her attendants, and she had so many of them. All the children from the commune had come to regard Ally as a kind of magical aunt. This day seemed such a celebration for all of them that not to include the kids would have been a crime. So Marigold and Jody and David and Tommy and Deidre and Lilly and baby Dot were all dressed in truly splendid clothes—provided by an excited Tambrine Creek Ladies Guild with much twittering and with even more love.

They looked wonderful. They all looked wonderful.

And Darcy would look more wonderful still.

Ally couldn't see him yet. Sergeant Matheson was holding the big oak doors firmly shut until just the right moment, when he'd swing them wide to let the bride start her walk. But Ally could imagine how he'd look.

Darcy. Her love.

He looked younger, too, she thought. The lines of strain around his eyes had eased. She was working beside him as a doctor now, sharing the burden that no longer seemed a burden. Medicine was fun. Life was fun.

She was still giving massages, but only to special clients—clients her mother worried about, or clients who really wanted Ally.

Like Darcy.

He was her favourite client.

As she was his.

Never fall in love with your clients, she thought. First rule of medicine. First rule of massage.

Too late. She'd fallen for him and the only way to make the whole thing equitable had been to have him massage her in return.

Luckily he was a very fast learner.

It was just perfect, she thought. Perfect.

Even the news of Jerry was good. He'd recover, which meant that Kevin could be cared for as a psychiatric patient without the stigma of murder to make his carers treat him with fear. Jerry himself was facing the first of many court cases. He'd be in jail for a very long time.

But enough of Jerry. He could be forgotten as a bad memory—a nightmare of a past that could no longer affect their future.

The music was starting now. Mendelssohn's Wedding March was being played—appallingly— by Doris on the church's hundred-year-old organ. It didn't matter.

Nothing mattered.

The doors were swinging wide. Her twitter of excited pageboys and flower girls started throwing rose petals, and her mother squeezed her hand.

'Are you ready, love?'

Ally smiled at her mother. Then she lifted her head and gazed down the long church aisle.

Darcy was waiting for her.

Darcy was smiling. He was smiling and smiling. Her love. Her future.

'I'm ready,' she whispered, and took her first step forward to her beloved. 'Let's begin.'

MEDICAL ROMANCE™

Large Print
Titles for the next six months...

January

THE CELEBRITY DOCTOR'S PROPOSAL Sarah Morgan
UNDERCOVER AT CITY HOSPITAL Carol Marinelli
A MOTHER FOR HIS FAMILY   Alison Roberts
A SPECIAL KIND OF CARING   Jennifer Taylor

February

HOLDING OUT FOR A HERO   Caroline Anderson
HIS UNEXPECTED CHILD   Josie Metcalfe
A FAMILY WORTH WAITING FOR   Margaret Barker
WHERE THE HEART IS   Kate Hardy

March

THE ITALIAN SURGEON   Meredith Webber
A NURSE'S SEARCH AND RESCUE   Alison Roberts
THE DOCTOR'S SECRET SON   Laura MacDonald
THE FOREVER ASSIGNMENT   Jennifer Taylor

MILLS & BOON®

Live the emotion

1205 LP 2P P1 Medic

MEDICAL ROMANCE™

Large Print

April

BRIDE BY ACCIDENT — Marion Lennox
COMING HOME TO KATOOMBA — Lucy Clark
THE CONSULTANT'S SPECIAL RESCUE — Joanna Neil
THE HEROIC SURGEON — Olivia Gates

May

THE NURSE'S CHRISTMAS WISH — Sarah Morgan
THE CONSULTANT'S CHRISTMAS PROPOSAL — Kate Hardy
NURSE IN A MILLION — Jennifer Taylor
A CHILD TO CALL HER OWN — Gill Sanderson

June

GIFT OF A FAMILY — Sarah Morgan
CHRISTMAS ON THE CHILDREN'S WARD — Carol Marinelli
THE LIFE SAVER — Lilian Darcy
THE NOBLE DOCTOR — Gill Sanderson

MILLS & BOON®

Live the emotion

1205 LP 2P P2 Medical